You won't believe it could happen today—this story will prove that it does. . . .

"Hit her again."

Sylvia did. Phyllis felt blood in her nose. She held back tears until they started to mingle with the blood. The walls were alive with cries of all the mortal girls like her. She imagined a ship moving toward her in the night. A slave ship.

"Good," said Barrezia.

"She's getting blood on my floor." Sylvia let Phyllis go to the polished cork all in a crumple. Phyllis was naked and bleeding upon it darkly.

"Best you wax it."

"You have to wax cork," said Sylvia Barnes. "Or else it stains . . ."

CRIED THE PIPER

by John Simmons

A DELL/EMERALD BOOK

Published by
Dell Publishing Co., Inc.
1 Dag Hammarskjold Plaza
New York, New York 10017

Dell ® TM 681510, Dell Publishing Co., Inc.

ISBN: 0-440-01549-9

Printed in the United States of America

First printing—November, 1983

Grateful acknowledgment is made to the following for permission
to reprint copyrighted material:
Rockaway Music Corp.: Two verses from the song "Loving
Machine" by. O. O. Merritt and D. Lambert. (p. 39) Copyright
© 1952 Rockaway Music Corp. Used by permission.

James Wiggins: One verse from the song "Gotta Shave 'Em Dry"
by James "Boodle It" Wiggins. (pp. 84–85) Recorded January
1930. Paramount 12916.

Piedmont Music Co.: Refrain from the song "Show Me the Way
To Go Home" by Irving King. (p. 259) Copyright © 1925 Harms,
Inc. Used by permission.

for ffk

A complete and detailed account of the shameless traffic in young girls by which the procurers and panders lure innocent young girls away from home and sell them to the keepers of dives. The magnitude of the organization and its workings. How to combat this hideous monster. How to save YOUR GIRL. How to save YOUR BOY. What you can do to help wipe out this curse of humanity. A book designed to awaken the sleeping and protect the innocent.

> —*Fighting the Traffic in Young Girls*, or *The War on the White Slave Trade* (1910)

PART ONE

ONE

Although it is ungainly, the Williamsburg Bridge rises from Lower Manhattan and crosses the East River with a forceful presence. It lacks the rhythmic beauty of the Brooklyn Bridge and the charming mystical disorder of the Manhattan Bridge. It is grey and rusting. But when Leffert Lefferts Buck designed it, early in this century, at sixteen hundred feet it was the longest suspension bridge in the world.

The women who work Delancey Street cross the Williamsburg Bridge often, because their clients pick them up a few blocks from the approaches and don't have much time to spare. The ride takes eight minutes and costs from ten to twenty dollars.

When Sunshine called Lucas Jameson on the night of the last cold Sunday in March, she was at a booth outside a Delancey Street diner and gazing up at the Williamsburg Bridge. The lights on the tower blinked beneath the fog as she listened to the telephone ring. She was surprised when there was an answer, and so she said:

"You're back."

Lucas Jameson brought the pillow over his head and it muffled his response. But yes, he was back. Had been for three hours. Was feeling fine, except for a mild form of dysentery, jet lag, and mosquito bites. He felt excellent. He lay in his own bed, between sheets of muslin, and if he needed to throw up, it would be in his own bathroom.

"Where were you?"

"Nigeria." Lucas felt the cramps flare.

"What for?"

"*National Geographic* wanted me to report on head-hunting among the Ibusa."

"You're lying."

"Yes." He turned on his side and picked up the clock. Ten minutes to one. "I needed a vacation."

Sunshine gave a sarcastic, nasal laugh.

"I had a wonderful time."

"You should've gone Club Med," said Sunshine. "I did, and came back with thousands of beads. It does—"

"Beads?"

"Doesn't matter." Sunshine was suddenly impatient. "I'm outside Moisha's."

Yes—and in his mind's eye Lucas could see her on the street, dressed in her demure red leather bomber's jacket, with glitter high heels and lips of vermouth.

"I found something on the bridge."

"Let me guess," said Lucas. "Animal, mineral, or latex?"

"You son of a bitch."

"Let me sleep."

"No. Come over."

So Lucas now knew he was really back in New York. He hadn't felt sure before—with Manhattan dreamlike on the misty approach to Kennedy, and the pacific taxi ride, and the fantasy all the while of iron intestines.

"What did you find?"

"A little trouble. And you owe me a favor."

Lucas tried to think what it could be. "I do?"

"Yes." Her voice was tremulous now, and an insistent octave high. "Come over and you'll see."

Lucas returned the telephone to its cradle, and for a moment argued with it silently. Then, rubbing open his eyes and still mumbling to himself, he began to dress in the dark. He slipped into slacks and found a sweatshirt and gym shoes. From a bottle of two hundred on the nightstand he poured four aspirin and went into the kitchen. The refrigerator was empty. He ran the tap until the water was cold and no longer brown, then took the pills with a glass of water. He discovered he was thirsty and had another. "I prefer two glasses of water," he said to himself. He drank.

Idly, Lucas wondered if there was any more heroin in the apartment. There was not. This was a good thing, he decided—although not even three glasses of water and a dozen aspirin would make you feel that particular way. Water did not make you high, nor aspirin. Heroin . . . But there wasn't any.

No heroin in Nigeria, either, which had been a good reason for going there. Nigeria was a long way from Westchester County, which was where Lucas had first encountered H, as those women liked to call it. Lucas had got far from H and very far from Westchester. Oshogbo, Nigeria, was five thousand miles from New York.

Lucas Jameson had almost ruined his career, not to mention his health, when he had found a nest of women, bored and middle-aged, who did not play contract bridge. They lived in Scarsdale, White Plains, Vahalia. They were the addicts of Westchester County, and there was a mansion on Wellsfleet Drive that made the shooting galleries on Avenue C look like penny arcades. For` Lucas it was supposed to have been a diversion from more serious reporting. It had been. He had become an addict himself. His friend, Roscoe Gatling, had told him, "That's what I call real involvement."

And now Lucas remembered the favor he owed Sunshine.

She had been the first to peer into his eyes, to run a practiced hand up his sleeve. And after emptying his pockets of Life Savers, Tootsie Rolls, and Hershey bars, she told him:

"Good Christ, you're a junkie."

So even at one in the morning, even if he was half-dead and consumed by internal parasites, he supposed he owed a visit to Sunshine at her workplace. She had a little trouble; he wondered what it was. He donned a wool jacket and patted it for keys, took his cigarettes and lighter from the nightstand, and left his apartment. When he missed a lonesome cab heading south, he decided to walk. He crossed Lafayette Street and turned downtown.

His face, ashen from illness, would change color with the night air that was chasing the mist. His eyes would widen. Lucas Jameson had boyish features— big dark eyes, pouting lips—and nothing in them belied a naivete which he did not in fact possess. His hair was black. With his hands in pockets and head down, he looked like a walking stick out for a stroll on its own.

It was a cold, windy night on the bleak, empty streets that led to Delancey. A feeling stole over him—familiar and unnerving—of elemental disorder. It was how the primitive astronomer must have felt, Lucas thought, the one who, gazing at the sky on a cloudy night, asked: *Where have the stars gone? Who am I? Where am I going?*

As he turned onto Delancey, the Williamsburg Bridge lay before him like a steel tongue.

Moisha's Diner was awash in hot pants and the lingering smell of brandy. The women inside shuddered over lemon cake and their last tricks. When Lucas entered, they looked after him with eyes glazed. He nodded to those several he had somehow come to know and smiled innocently at others. Sunshine was in a corner in the back.

At twenty-five Sunshine was younger than many. Lucas had known her a couple of years. They drank together occasionally in a Canal Street bar, where Christian Brothers was poured into bottles of Hennessy

Sunshine told him stories with a flair for bitter detail; then after hours she beat him at pool. Neither generous nor pleasant, she needed this better company, and sometimes so did Lucas.

She stood and smiled when she saw him, or twisted her thin lips into uneasy shapes. She wore leather pants with the jacket, and beneath it was a pink sweater. Her blond hair fell awry.

"You look awful," she said.

"Thanks. Is that your little girl?"

"Don't be funny."

A girl not older than nine or ten was sitting at the table with Sunshine, dressed in a yellow rain slicker with the top down. Her brown hair was matted into a disheveled frame for a round cherubic face which was streaked with grime and into which dark eyes disappeared. Her hands were curled into fists in her lap.

"You found her on the bridge?"

Sunshine shrugged. "She was climbing onto the walkway. I followed her."

"Maybe she was going home."

"She huddled in a corner."

"Does she talk?"

"No. She can say that—no." Sunshine ran a bony hand through the girl's hair. "Her name's Vera."

Lucas warmed his tingling fingers with his breath. "If she won't talk, how do you know?"

Sunshine reached into the girl's lap and brought up a recalcitrant hand. She turned it over; on the wrist was the name, in blue and crudely drawn.

"It's a tattoo."

"And not a very good one."

"She drank some coffee," said Sunshine. "I gave her some eggs, but she threw up."

"There's a bug going around," said Lucas.

"She ran away from somebody," said Sunshine. "She's not lost."

"Ran away from who?"

"Who knows?"

"And you call me?"

"For a favor."

Lucas drank from Sunshine's coffee cup. "Why don't you tell the cops?"

"I don't like cops. I got a—what did you say once?"

"Abiding mistrust," said Lucas, replacing the green-rimmed cup in its saucer. "The Women's Shelter?"

"For bag ladies."

"Hospital, then. Bellevue."

Sunshine nodded, relieved. "Say it's child abuse. You take her."

Lucas reached over and laid two fingers against the child's forehead. It was cool.

"I've got to work," said Sunshine. "Take her with you now and tomorrow morning—"

"*I should take her?*"

"Please, Lucas?"

He felt a chill and looked around. Had he raised his voice? The counterman, the waitress, and the women were watching. They were unsmiling, but he smiled in haste. In the meantime Vera slipped quietly under the table.

"Get her, Lucas—"

"For God's sake." He reached for her below and fumbled with her hands, which were sticky and damp.

He pulled her out. She strained against him in her rubber coat. "You want to go with me?"

Vera said nothing. Then she said, "No."

"She doesn't mean it," said Sunshine. "Do you, honey?"

Vera thought for a moment, and said, "No."

Lucas Jameson was living in the Colonnades, a row of four once-fashionable townhouses near Astor Place. Washington Irving had lived in them once. A long time ago. He'd been dead for quite a while.

Lucas explained all this to Vera, who was silent. She asked no questions. She followed him obediently into the taxi on Delancey, and later followed him out. When she realized which door they were going in, she ran ahead and waited.

Lucas didn't know much about children. He was thirty-four years old, an only child, and had never been married. He lacked cousins. Occasionally he noticed children playing in the streets or walking with their mothers. They all seemed quite young. None seemed as quiet as Lucas remembered himself as a child. Except perhaps Vera, who waited silently while he unlocked the door to his apartment.

A dark form bounded through the hallway and out of sight as he swung open the door. Vera screamed.

"That was the cat," Lucas explained. "Don't scream. If you can find him, you can keep him. I haven't seen him in months."

Vera was guarded but looked after the cat curiously, the memory of a smile playing on her lips.

Lucas gestured to the apartment. "Say how nice it is. Someday I'm going to get some furniture."

She followed him down the long, broad hallway,

which led from the living room, or parlor, past the bedrooms and study. He had too much space. He wasn't responsible for the marble floor. "I don't know who was. John Jacob Astor. He went down with the *Titanic*."

In the bathroom Lucas ran water in the old sure-footed tub, and Vera knew exactly what to do. She took off all her clothes. She unzipped her rain slicker and pulled off a filthy purple dress. She took off her little shoes. That was all she wore.

Lucas got a towel and a wash cloth. "I don't have any bubble bath. Do you mind?"

"No." She climbed into the bath with the water still running and offered Lucas the bar of soap from the dish. "Wash me."

"That's good," said Lucas. " 'Wash me.' "

He hadn't given anybody a bath in a long time. He remembered when his mother used to give him baths, however. "She used to tell me about Joe McCarthy," he told Vera conversationally. "How he was beaming radio waves from the Empire State Building."

The girl was filthy. On her back were some welts, and together with dark bruises on her arms and legs, Vera's body was a study in black and blue.

"You've been knocked around, huh?"

"My name's Vera." She spread her lips to a little smile.

He tapped her temple with a finger. "Somebody's home."

"Wash my hair."

He did, and rinsed it, and rubbed it damp. Vera accepted these ministrations compliantly. In fact, the way she turned so easily under his hands and accom-modated him with half-smiles hinted at intimacy. It was peculiar; it was feigned. Lucas lifted her out of the bath.

"Time for bed," she said.

She raised her arms so that he could draw the towel around her and, as he dried her back, moved toward him. Her arms snaked around his neck; she preened for him and teased him with a cheesecake smile.

"Time for bed," she repeated. Her eyes had become vacant.

Lucas let the towel drop and disentangled himself. He felt suddenly uncomfortable. He closed his eyes to pinch the bridge of his nose.

"No?"

"Enough," said Lucas. He shook his head. "First, you take the cushions off the couch. Throw them in the corner, then find the handle, and pull. It's a Castro Convertible."

She stepped back and stood ready to pirouette.

"Even a child can do it." He smiled. "Can you dance?"

She nodded and put on airs.

"Well, dance into the living room."

Vera put a finger to her lips.

"Thataway," pointed Lucas. He picked her dress off the floor. "I'll put you to bed in a minute."

Vera bowed and went spinning.

Lucas ran some water in the sink and started to soak the dress. It was only good manners. At Bellevue they wouldn't care if he brought in a lost kid in a mud pie of a dress. It was not that sort of hospital. But he poured in half a bottle of Woolite. In a few minutes he would take it out, hang it up to dry, and iron it in the morning. If he could find the iron. Better damp than dirty.

Suddenly the cat came flying into the bathroom in a rage, scrambling insanely onto the bathtub with its back up. Crying.

"It's just a little girl," said Lucas.

Hudson was not a likable cat. It was an angry, disenchanted cat with worn stripes, yet still a good mouser. It stood on the bathtub vibrating.

"She's just your age," said Lucas. He dragged the dress out of the water. He knew he wasn't supposed to wring it out. "About ten and she's—"

He stepped quickly to the doorway.

Little girl Vera was running and slipping, her bare feet arrhythmic on the cold marble. Her face was contorted. She was naked and awkward, her arms spread wide, and she was screaming.

When he saw the shotgun, Lucas dropped hard to his knees. Into the hallway stepped a man in a khaki coat, an amorphous face atop his shoulders. It was a Halloween mask.

Scrambling in panic, Vera was about to be assassinated. Lucas lunged for her. Her last screams echoed in the cavernous hallway and were drowned out by the single, shattering blast.

TWO

Word of what had happened to the little girl named Vera went out on the lips of baby pros. It whistled along Eighth Avenue, turned on 42nd Street and headed for Lex, spread through the Lower East Side and uptown as far as Harlem east and central. Lucas Jameson stared at the ceiling in St. Vincent's Hospital.

"It was the Piper."

Roscoe Gatling smiled. "That's chipmunk talk."

Sunshine had brought Lucas that news, with flowers, and the daisies lay dying at his bedside. He remembered only that she said, "On the street they say that's the Piper."

"Chipmunks," said Gatling.

Young prostitutes seemed to think—though no special consensus was taken—that Vera had been killed at the behest of a mythic slaver. The Piper was part of the lore of the street. He was vicious. He snatched little match girls, and not for their matches. The duds he eliminated.

"Are they right?" asked Lucas.

"Chipmunks are smart."

Roscoe Gatling found the button that raised the head of the hospital bed. He was now, had always been, the most thoughtful homicide detective Lucas had ever met. He was a small, wiry man with prematurely white hair and sideburns bending past his ears. His wife had had a nervous breakdown a while back, and since then he spent Saturdays feeding pigeons in Union Square, humming 'Round Midnight and doing all the solos himself. Lucas had known him ever since they met at the scene of an icepick murder in Hell's Kitchen. They had become friends despite The New York Times, for which Lucas had worked a brief while.

"Who sent that?" On the way up Lucas saw the basket of apples, tangerines, chestnuts, and fruitcake.

"Westchester florist," said Gatling. "No card."

"Somebody's still grateful . . ." That he'd been too high to remember her name when he wrote the article titled "Flying to Scarsdale."

The bed reached a forty-degree angle and Gatling stopped it. "Ever hear Coltrane play Ascension?"

"Never."

"Well, you almost did. The shell was packed with pellets and broken glass."

Lucas felt the tightening of bandages across his upper chest as he raised white adhesive arms. Gauze covered one side of his neck and chin.

Vera had been killed. Lucas only remembered diving for her, and missing.

Gatling pulled up a plastic chair. "She was actually eleven years old. Ivory Phipps had bought her. Ivory is a pimp."

"Bought her?" Lucas accepted the cigarette that Gatling inserted in his mouth.

"Ivory beat his traffic tickets for this," nodded Gatling. "She was delivered to him for $25,000 and was supposed to be patient with older men."

"She wasn't."

"Ivory chalked it up to quality control. She ran away."

"He didn't kill her?"

Gatling recoiled in mock astonishment. "He wears a flea collar, but that's about all."

"How did Ivory get her?"

"He called up." Gatling reached into the fruit basket and picked out a tangerine. He bit off the top and peeled it.

"Called who?"

Gatling shrugged. He put the half-peeled tangerine to his ear. "I want a little girl. Blonde, if you have it. Not too chatty, no chest and no heartaches. This is Ivory Phipps and I have more money than Ritz got crackers. My Master Charge number is—"

"Where's the phone?"

"A bar in Pittsburgh, gas station in Providence,

dry cleaner's in Rochester.'' Gatling pulled the tangerine apart and ate it in sections with loud sucking noises. ''Vera Doe—age eleven—bought by professional procurer and pimp named Phipps from an unknown vendor.''

''Child prostitution—''

''White slavery, they used to call it when I was a boy.''

''I didn't think they had that any more.'' Lucas gazed along his arms and down his nose at the bandages. He might be wrong.

''You're out of step with the times, Lucas.'' Gatling rose and kicked the plastic chair into the corner. ''It's coming back.''

''It must be against the law,'' said Lucas. Buying and selling children. Shooting them. It could not be legal and therefore must have run directly into the investigative arms of—

''The FBI isn't interested,'' said Gatling. ''It's not the Mafia. Good Italian families are into straight—do you mind if I say blowjob?''

''No.''

''Into straight blowjobs, not this. Child porn, yes; peep shows, yes. But not this.''

''This is too sick,'' declared Lucas, off-key.

''Sick? Who said anything about sick?'' Gatling went to stare out the window. It was a sunny day. ''Slavery is a great American tradition. It's just not a growth industry.''

''And this girl's murder—I suppose that's out of your zone.''

''Third Homicide Zone is interested in any murder between 14th and 58th Street. The kid was shot in the first zone. But no, they're not too interested either. It's a good thing—''

"I just got back from Nigeria," announced Lucas. The cigarette, still in his mouth, was extinguished at the filter. He spit it out. "I'm on assignment for the *National Geogr*—"

"I was just telling them down at the morgue how lucky it's got to be for that little dead girl that somebody like you—"

"Head-hunting among the Ibusa."

Gatling turned from the window as one of the Catholic sisters rolled in the needle cart. She prepared a syringe.

"They don't dress them the way they used to, do they?"

"No," agreed Lucas.

"New habits but the same old crap."

The nun ignored that. She said sweetly, "I'm going to take some of your blood, Mr. Jameson."

"You don't have a choice, Lucas." Gatling picked up a shiny green apple.

"This arm. For Christ's sake." Lucas winced. "What do you mean—no choice?"

"You're next," said Gatling.

The cloistered nurse withdrew the needle from the engauzed arm and pressed it with a swab. She held up the syringe to the light. "That's a good healthy color," she said.

Gatling bit into his apple. "They'll be coming after you now."

THREE

Jonathan Barnes returned to Palm Beach on the last night coach from New York. He was tired and hungry, and an outlaw headache strapped his skull. It had taken four days rather than two. His single white shirt had not been enough and was plastered to his back. His suit was wrinkled. And when he saw the glimmer of airport lights, they didn't bid him welcome but seemed to jeer: "So you're back."

Sylvia was waiting for him. For two hours she had been sitting in the Cadillac running down the battery, reading the *Enquirer* and eating peanut brittle. They began to bicker at once over nothing and ended the night by not speaking. At home, Jonathan undressed and went to sleep. He waked to the radio at seven the next morning, and lay listening to it for an hour.

His headache was gone, but he treated himself gingerly lest it return. He showered for a long time, soaping his slender body twice over, and when he patted the flesh dry, it was pink and warm. Then he shaved with a new blue blade. Two days' growth of beard came off like so much grime.

At thirty-six, age was beginning to soften his features, a fact which Jonathan noticed every morning with detached concern. Fatty tissue was gathering around his bony chin and bags were filling below his eyes. His light brown hair was thinner and streaked with grey.

Sylvia had laid out his clothes, a pair of sky-blue Bermuda shorts and a red and white checked shirt. Jonathan put them on, slipped into sandals, and padded downstairs. In the kitchen Sylvia was prattling about making bacon and eggs. Her red hair was in curlers, the black roots showing. Her face was smeared with cream. Jonathan sat down and, when she served him, began to eat methodically. He read the newspaper and ignored the steady stream of small talk.

"I said—" She laid the last strip of bacon on his plate to get his attention. "I went to the dog races yesterday."

He nodded. "Did you win?"

"I lost twenty." She sat down before toast. "Did you get to Kiehl's?"

"Not this time."

"I wanted some more of that lotion." She scraped the burnt part of the toast with her knife.

"You certainly need it."

"What's that supposed to mean?"

While Jonathan examined critically the last piece of bacon, the doorbell rang.

"Who's that?" asked Sylvia.

"Why don't you answer it and find out?"

She got up, tightening her robe and glaring. She felt her curlers and damned herself as she went through the hallway to the front door. Soon Jonathan heard her gushing and knew it was Barrezia. He rifled the newspaper for the comics.

"Now doesn't this man look pretty today, Jonathan?" Sylvia adopted her antebellum accent.

Luis Barrezia nodded hello and Jonathan inclined his head. The Cuban's olive complexion was relaxed and he smiled with mild forebearance. His broad face, once darkly handsome, was aging to drooping circles. His black eyes darted beneath their sleepy lids. Below them lay a flat nose and a long, glistening mouth. He was tall and fat; thirty pounds gained in the last year made him top three hundred.

Beside him Sylvia looked petite and fawning. "I'll bet that suit's all linen and custom made."

The Cuban reacted like a big bear in tails; he pawed at the knot of his tie. Sylvia reached up and touched the small gold shield on his lapel. "What's that little thing you've got there?"

"Battle of Giron," mumbled Barrezia, grinning. "Bay of Pigs."

Jonathan didn't listen. He had known the man standing in the doorway for twenty years.

"I bet Havana's nice this time of year," said Sylvia.

"Very nice. Excellent."

"Why don't you go back, then?" Jonathan smiled thinly, peering over his reading glasses.

Sylvia left the Cuban's side and poured him a cup of coffee. "Jonathan," she clucked. "He got in late last night," she said apologetically, "and he's just been impossible."

Barrezia accepted the coffee standing. "Yes? Impossible?"

"He certainly is." Sylvia returned the milk to the refrigerator. "And I made him a big breakfast, too."

Jonathan closed and folded the paper, and then, removing his glasses, he caught the other man's eyes. They seemed deep and full of love. Between them there was an awkward moment of silence. Sylvia noticed it and began to load the dishwasher.

"We'll go upstairs," said Jonathan quietly.

"I'm going to vacuum up there, honey." She had heard him over the clatter she was making. "Why don't you go in the den?"

Jonathan watched Sylvia flutter with the box of detergent. He twisted his napkin and rose.

"Yes, Jonathan," smiled Barrezia. "The den."

Jonathan stiffened at a tone in the Cuban's voice. "I'll get my briefcase," he said.

A low-ceilinged, wood-paneled room built off the garage, Jonathan's den was full of memories, none of which meant much to him. Sylvia had designed the room, had had it built, and had installed all the knick-knacks. He didn't care about his bronzed baby shoes or his silver spoon. He would have liked to burn his pink, lace-covered baby book—but it stood, faded and peeling, on the false mantelpiece. All his childhood pictures highlighted the fact that he was still round-shouldered and skinny, and he longed to consign them to flames, along with his university degree, which hung on the wall, laminated in plastic wood. He cringed inwardly when he saw it. It was flanked by the two framed awards for Math Teacher of the Year, won in two successive and dreadful years at Boca Raton High School. What had he done to deserve them? He couldn't remember.

In the whole clutter of dejected recollection there was only one thing that Jonathan cared for. That was his old Spaulding catcher's mask, which sat atop the battered rolltop desk. He had worn it when he played baseball in high school, and even then it had had a curious appeal. When he was angry or upset, he still sometimes liked to put it on.

Barrezia was already in the den when Jonathan came in. He was fingering the baby shoes, as he often did. He turned to Jonathan grinning:

"Speech!"

"No, not today. We have important—"

"Speeches to make, yes?" The Cuban tossed the baby shoes back on the mantel. "Important—"

"No!" Jonathan twisted uncomfortably in his chair.

Barrezia withdrew a small lavender chapbook from the inside pocket of his jacket. The book was ragged and dog-eared; he thrust it onto the desk.

"I won't do it." Jonathan laid both his hands flat on the desk. Then they panicked.

Barrezia was swift. He caught one of the retreating hands. At first he held it gently in his own. *"Read."*

"No."

With his free hand Barrezia opened the book. The text was mutilated. Whole passages were blotted out. Pages were torn.

It always happened this way. It had started many years before as a game. Barrezia was always so angry at Castro. Who could blame him? He could never return to his homeland. Jonathan and he had liked to play games together—such as this. Barrezia still did. *"Read!"*

"Ridiculous," breathed Jonathan.

First came the tightening. Jonathan clenched his teeth.

"You want big cigar," grinned Barrezia. "You look just like Fidel. I put big cigar in mouth."

There was the painful constriction now. Jonathan drew his lips back in agony. The pain began to radiate. The Cuban's smile broadened. Jonathan half-rose from his chair. There was a point past which he couldn't go. Tears dropped onto the pages of the book. Choking, he began to read.

"Only death can liberate me from such misery!"

"Excellent!" Barrezia squeezed tighter still. "Go on. *Society is moved to compassion . . ."*

". . . upon hearing of the kidnapping or murder of one child, but they are criminally indifferent to the mass murder . . ."

Barrezia laughed. He began pulling at Jonathan's hair. "Really, Fidel, you are doing very well today."

He began to mash Jonathan's small pink fingers, rolling them like chopsticks between his own. He turned the pages randomly and pointed again. As

Jonathan's head bobbed on the desk, Barrezia picked it up by the hair.

"The markets should be overflowing . . ."

"Louder!" Barrezia pulled up the hand between his fist. It was beet red and looked like it could explode. He plucked at the knuckles. "Much louder!"

"Pantries should be full!" Jonathan began to scream petulantly. *"All hands should be working! This is not an inconceivable thought."*

Jonathan stumbled through the text. With his free hand he turned the book on its face and opened it from the back. As Barrezia began the final pumping motions, he found it and cried: *"I don't care! History—"*

"Yes! *History will absolve me!*"

The Cuban tossed back the hand he had crushed.

"You son of a bitch," whispered Jonathan.

Barrezia took out a folded handkerchief and patted his forehead. "I just squeeze a little."

Jonathan had never fainted. Once he had tried to bite Barrezia, but for that got his mouth opened in an unusual way. Now he swallowed his tears and watched his hand begin to uncurl.

It wasn't the agony that bothered him, so much as the fact that the game of "Castro Speaks" recalled to him that the give-and-take of their friendship was in great part gone, perhaps forever. Barrezia could squeeze his hand, but Jonathan was no longer allowed to drag his fingernails across the big man's chest and make the nipples bloody. They no more went striding through Miami, searching for bulldogs to torture. It had been ten years since Jonathan had provoked a young musclebound in a wayside bar and led him outside to where Barrezia was waiting in the shadows.

Jonathan often longed for those early days of their friendship. They had met when Jonathan was just out of high school; the Cuban was the older by a dozen years. From the start they had been curiously inseparable—the boy with barely peach fuzz on his upper lip and the swarthy Latin American approaching thirty. Because people didn't know what they shared—and they didn't either, for that matter—there often were rumors that they were homosexuals. Such groundless and maddening gossip they squelched at every opportunity, and were it not such calumny, they'd have found it laughable.

Despite the loss of excitement, however, Jonathan knew that in many ways their bonding—for it was less a relationship than that, a bonding—was even stronger today. Their lives were entwined by more than adolescent palaver. What they had lost in exquisite pleasure, they had gained in substance and devotion. At least Jonathan wanted to think so.

Barrezia lay down on the old leather couch; his bulk hung over the side. "Why was he not killed?"

Jonathan sighed. "He should have been, of course. But you just paid for the girl."

"Fool—"

"You gave me two thousand dollars," said Jonathan. "It's not enough any more. For that price I get creeps."

"That is obvious. Who is this Lucky Jimsom?" Barrezia wrote a headline with his finger and framed the tabloid with his hands. "LUCKY JIMSOM KILLS GIRL, SELF."

"With a shotgun?"

Barrezia shrugged. "Cannot kill him now so easy."

Jonathan shivered. In New York he had been packing his bags when the news came on the radio. It was good at first; then it was bad. The girl was dead. But Lucas Jameson was alive. And worse: he didn't turn out to be a baker or banker or dry cleaner. Jonathan had stayed up all night waiting to hear that he had died. He didn't die, didn't even come close.

"Let's not argue," said Jonathan quietly.

"I no argue." The Cuban grunted and laid his hands behind his head. "Let's hear it."

Jonathan withdrew a manila folder from his briefcase, swiveled up in his chair, then opened it on his lap. It represented two extra days in New York. Barrezia liked these case histories.

"Lucky Jimsom. Tell me about Lucky."

"Lucas Jameson. American journalist, thirty-four years old. Born in Tacoma, Washington. Mother Evelyn, unstable. Nervous breakdown when Jameson was six. Institutionalized and still lives—Dx paranoid schizophrenia—in a Seattle mental hospital."

"Very rare," observed Barrezia. "True paranoia is very unusual."

"Father, William. Died last year. Owner of a ticking factory."

"Ticking?"

"Beds." Jonathan saw Barrezia nod with misunderstanding. "Not sex, just cases for mattresses."

Barrezia grinned.

"As a child he was a discipline problem. Attended military schools. Left college after two years. Moved to New York in 1968. Four days as a police reporter in 1969 for the *Post*. Fired for wearing Viet Cong flag on his lapel. Lasted at *The New York Times* three months. Wrote a book in 1971 called *A Flame for Charlie*, which is supposed to be a black account of six Americans and three Buddhist monks who immolated themselves as a form of protest—''

"Magnificent!" exclaimed Barrezia. He half raised up. "He wrote this?"

"I thought you'd like that," nodded Jonathan. "The people who poured kerosene all over themselves and—"

"Yes, yes, I know. Did you get a copy?"

"It's out of print."

"See if you can find it," said Barrezia. "Go on."

"It set the tone for everything else. Derelict murders in Denver; the Salamander nightclub disaster; the Saigon airlift where the plane crashed and the children were killed—"

"Ah," said Barrezia.

"Wrote a syndicated column for a year which was a flop. He said himself that, 'Writing for an American newspaper is like trying to feed an autistic child. No amount of milk or attention can ever elicit the impression that one is actually communicating with another.' "

"Autistic child—"

"I don't know what it means, either."

"Form of child schizophrenia," said Barrezia. "If it weren't for Castro—"

"I know," said Jonathan, "you'd be Sigmund Freud."

"No psychiatrists in Cuba. I'd be doctor."

"Yeah, just look at your white suit," said Jonathan. "Want to hear the punch line?"

Barrezia frowned.

"A year ago he dropped out of sight. Six months later he publishes some wild stories on housewife narcotics addicts in suburbia. Hasn't been heard from since. Rumors are that he's drinking, or going paranoid like his mother."

The Cuban turned on his side, taking care not to wrinkle his suit. "Tell me."

"I found out. What's your guess?"

"I no guess," grinned Barrezia. "No amount of milk—hah!" He stretched languidly and added, "He addict himself."

Jonathan's face fell. He closed the folder and tossed it on the desk. "He was chipping at first. It got serious. He quit by himself and took a vacation."

Barrezia raised his feet and sat up. "What about this punch line? What you think?"

"Maybe he's washed—"

"Bullshit. Trouble. He come after us for sure. You must do something."

Jonathan glanced at his catcher's mask.

"I want you to go back to New York."

"Again?"

"Listen—" Barrezia leaned forward. "I give you ten thousand dollars. No. More." He raised two fingers. "I want you do one thing and another."

There was a sudden rattling at the door. Barrezia put a finger to his mouth and sat up straight and grinned.

Sylvia came in. She had put on a dress and taken down her hair. Into the den she walked bearing a

silver tray with a pot of coffee, apple slices, a chunk
of Swiss cheese, and Triscuits.

"I thought you boys—"

"Mother," snapped Jonathan, "can't you see we're
talking?"

FOUR

The Venus Lounge was a step-down tavern on Eleventh Avenue in the West Forties. It was a grim warehouse district. A hand-painted sign hung from the fire escape, with the word *Lounge* scripted over a pale blue planet. A rusty iron railing ran along the three steps down and met a heavy wooden door.

Roscoe Gatling had told Lucas to go there, and he arrived at three in the afternoon on a cold spring

day. Nobody took Lucas's coat at the checkroom.
The place was narrow and dark. He sat down at the
end of a long, empty bar. The piano, a baby grand,
was on a low platform behind him. He ordered a
martini without vermouth, and said to the chubby,
rueful bartender:

"She's supposed to meet me."

"Not up yet, but she'll be down in a while." The
bartender started tumbling glasses into soapy water
and rinsing them beneath the faucet.

Lucas was waiting for an old woman named Louise Cole, who owned the Venus Lounge and the
rooming house above it. The rooming house, though
not the Barbizon or Longacre, was meant exclusively
for young women. It was not a cathouse, but many of
the girls who lived there had come from the brothels
around town or from the street. They were escaping
pimps, drugs, parents, or the police. Louise did not
ask for references.

"You ought to go see her," Gatling had told him.

"I will."

"Now listen to this."

Louise Cole had been a singer during the 1920s,
when she still was a teenager, and Gatling played for
Lucas her old blues records. She had a high, trembling
voice which rose against the strident rhythms of a
solo piano—barrelhouse, Gatling called it. Lucas,
who seldom liked music, listened to the tapes Gatling
brought every day before he was released from the
hospital.

"It's too bad you missed Easter," the old homicide detective told him. "She don't play much any-
more besides then."

On every Easter Sunday, Louise played for old friends. For a chorus she gathered the girls who stayed upstairs around her piano. She played old standards like *Nobody's Business* and *Shave 'Em Dry*, but one song Lucas would have liked to hear had an original refrain. Louise always set it up with a tinkling introduction:

"This is an old song that'll make the women remember and the men recognize what's it like to be a girl in hard hard times. . . ."

And she would take off with quarter notes hacked into eighths because she never could leave boogie-woogie behind. She'd sing:

> *You put a nickel in the slot*
> *Hear somethin' buzzin'*
> *Kisses come hot*
> *At five cents a dozen . . .*

And the girls would sing the chorus:

> *But don't send me to the Piper*
> *Don't send me to the Piper*
> *He's too mean to me.*

Louise would fall away laughing and come back:

> *You put a nickel in the slot*
> *Things light up*
> *Out comes your lovin'*
> *In a Dixie Cup . . .*

And with that the girls would cry:

Don't send me down the Pipeline
But don't send me down the Pipeline
He's too fat for me!

There were twenty verses in all, including the improvisations which began to build after the first ten.

"It's better than these disco jerks," said Gatling. "Anytime."

Louise Cole walked with a cane. She was small-framed and slightly stooped. As she passed along the bar, she told the bartender, "Remy, Darlin'."

And light-skinned; in Mississippi she would be high yellow. Her beauty still was in her eyes, which were soft ovals spreading warmth into a thin, deeply lined face. Her hair was nappy. She wore a long-sleeved black dress that would have buttoned but was open at the throat. She hooked her cane on the bar, then offered Lucas a sculpted hand with hardened fingers.

"I never had a chance to read your column, Mr. Jameson," she said. "Roscoe told me about it."

"You weren't the only one," said Lucas. "It died a natural death."

"That's about the best kind, isn't it?" The old woman sipped her cognac.

"I suppose so."

"Not like that—what was her name?"

"Vera."

"They're all named that in recent days." Louise shook her head. "No trunk or clothes, don't even know their own name. Scared of shadows, won't say nothing."

"That was her."

"And a tattooed wrist."

"Yes."

"Got you, too, Roscoe said."

"My shoulders are tight." Lucas tried to shrug.

"You're just lucky." Louise Cole finished her drink. "That would be the Piper."

Lucas drained his own glass and waved to the bartender.

"With me it was Big Chief."

"Big Ch—"

"They're all the same," said Louise, shaking her head. "I was fifteen years old in 1929. Had left my home in Clarksdale, Mississippi. Traveled to Grafton, Wisconsin, to record for Paramount Records."

"*Cast Iron Blues, Tabletop Blues, Dead Rider* . . ."

"And many others which they failed to release," nodded Louise with muted pleasure. "But it was my first and last opportunity to have my name on record. Because in Chicago, the next day, I got lost. Outside the De Luxe Cafe on 35th and State. Ma Rainey was playing there, and the boys went in without me. She didn't like no competition."

"Lost on the streets?" asked Lucas.

"I walked them all night long. I was a country girl. Didn't know a back alley from a cotton patch. By daybreak I met a man who did something to me that I kept the rest of my life. . . ."

Louise Cole laid her forearm on the bar, unbuttoned the sleeve of her dress, and let her wrist fall out.

It was a tattoo. Drawn quite as crudely as the one on Vera's wrist. It was faded by age, but if Lucas could have peered closer, he might have made it out. The etiquette of tattoo-gazing intervened. Louise let her arm fall abruptly and rebuttoned her sleeve. She said:

"That same kind of men. Some pass along history by writing books, Mr. Jameson."

Lucas fumbled for cigarettes. "There are other ways," he acknowledged.

"Yes. I was luckier than most, I suppose. They sent me somewhere—to this day I believe it was Southern Indiana. Poor country, but near some big gambling joint. Strange name. French something."

"French Lick," nodded Lucas. "A resort in the twenties. Still a hotel."

"Red devil at the entrance?"

"Hot water springs," nodded Lucas. "That's the one."

"I was taken there for men several times. Trained nearby. Everybody called the man who had me Big Chief. All of 'em have places to train you."

"Even today?"

"What? You think times change?" Louise shrugged and pushed her snifter into the gutter of the bar. "It ain't no different. Girl has to be broken. How about a Remy, Mr. Jameson?"

He agreed. As soon as she raised her finger the bartender came with the bottle.

"They shipped me back North and sold me to a pimp. An old cadet named Murphy. Pimps used to call themselves cadets—did you know that?"

"No."

"But they was pimps all the same. Treated me brutal. I don't think I need to show you, Mr. Jameson.

My old Murphy was so bad he used a whip. Give me narcotics any day, I'm telling you. He was so low-down to the core that—'' Louise suddenly snapped her head up, "That a woman shot him dead and I run like hell.''

She began to laugh, putting her head down and leaning away from the bar. She had an infectious laugh, from deep in her throat. Lucas couldn't help himself. She grasped his wrist with one hand and wiped tears from her eyes with the other.

"Big goddamned whore white woman with black and blue chin, half one ear gone. I was there and she come in and say, 'All right, Murphy, you get . . . *this!*' '' Louise made a pistol of her fingers and fired it. "I was just a little thing—you see me now—and I looked up and just said, '*Yuh gwine shoot me, too, Miz Beth?*' ''

Lucas picked up both their glasses and gave Louise hers.

"Pig *dirty* motherfucker—toast his guts,'' laughed Louise.

They drank.

"I was more on my own after that. I stayed a whore in the thirties. Today I got to credit Al Capone. He taught me how to read and write—so's ah doan speaks lak dis.''

"Al Capone?''

"The gangsters. They ran things in Chicago then. I suppose they still do. It was the depression, you know. So there was a big supply of hookers. So many of us, mighty of fact, that they wouldn't let us work but three days a week. So the other four I went to—I believe it was called Mrs. Wellsey's School of Advancement for Young Ladies.''

Louise drummed on the bar. "You see what this brandy does to lubricate my throat, Mr. Jameson? Maybe I ought to try some Perrier water to constrict it."

The bartender was already uncapping a small green bottle.

"Besides, you're a white man and maybe you can tell me why I pay fifty cents for six ounces of water that gives you kidney stones."

"I don't think—"

"Yeah, you're not French. The French have mouths specially shaped for it." Louise pointed to her glass. "Drop some bitters in it, darlin'."

"You could start a world war that way."

"I started the last one." She drank. "Ever been married?"

Lucas shook his head.

"That's smart. But I tell you, in 1939 I got a man. He was a doctor, a general practitioner, tall as a skyscraper and black like me. We married and came here, to New York. He sold his father's mansion on old South Parkway, and when we boarded the Twenti-eth Century Limited—you know what he said to me?"

Lucas couldn't guess.

"He was a good man. He said, 'If you think we're leaving Chicago on account of your past, my dear, I just want you to know that I love Harlem in the fall and people in the dusky sash are sick as anyplace else.' "

Louise Cole suppressed a girlish laugh. In a sud-den movement she reached over the bar and poured her water in the sink. The loyal bartender was on his way with the Remy.

"He died about 1950. I still got all his books upstairs. They're full of things about diseases and such. Every disease you want. Except maybe the one we're talking about."

"Except that one," said Lucas. "Yes."

They moved to a table in the back as the afternoon wore on. The Venus Lounge caught customers escaping work, and by five in the afternoon they talked below a squall of conversation. She was all that Gatling had promised; she was more. She absorbed him so thoroughly that he almost forgot why he had come. Yet, as the light through the transom faded, the fundamental reason lingered in his gut. But that business—and it was hardly business, for she asked nothing herself in return—took only a moment.

"White slavery, Mr. Jameson. But not so very white, I can tell you. What will you do?"

"I need help," he admitted.

"You need bait," she said, "don't you?"

"Yes."

"I don't have anything now." Louise shook her head. "But sometime soon."

"How will I know?"

"I'll write you a note."

He inclined his head for thanks.

"And Mr. Jameson . . ."

He foresaw what she would say. Why was he doing this? *Why, Mr. Jameson, you want to get messed up in this?* So he had lived and somebody was letting out a contract; so what? Why not a long vacation? Nigeria—Ibusa—honorary tribesman. Before she could ask him, he was telling her:

"I detest myself."

FIVE

Thoroughly. The internal world of Lucas Jameson was in shambles. It had been for several years. When he waked in the morning and remembered who he was, it was as though a mental cattle prod was being used on his brain. If he shaved—and it seemed that shaving preserved a civilized visage—he perforce looked at himself in the mirror. And was disgusted.

Lucas did not know how to explain it. His self-esteem was like a smooth rock covered with the slime of some fundamental psychological muck. Air could not reach it; it was not accessible to the real world. He did not recall when it had begun—when his head had become a self-slaughterhouse—but he presumed it was out of his past. His father had been a gentle man who hated himself for making profits off mattress ticking. His mother had projected her wish for love onto others, and it returned as delusions of persecution. He knew, in short, that he had a past, but he ignored it. He kept meaning to try psychoanalysis but never had.

In fact, Lucas Jameson was honest enough. He had most of the ordinary virtues. He subscribed to some vague moral code which they taught in military academies, and he never breached it, except to get a story. He shared the view of his own detestability with only a few critics. They asked the same question he did. What kind of man liked, or was compelled, to write about the self-immolation of Buddhist monks, nightclub fires, the horrible deaths of Vietnamese children? *One learns to live with the smell of burning flesh*, he had written, naively, in *A Flame for Charlie*. But who seeks it out?

Now—child prostitution? It seemed to Lucas, finally, apt. After the narcotics addiction he had wondered how low he could go. The question was not how to top his previous work, but into what miserable depths he could descend. He would have preferred to research the head-hunters of Ibusa. But he never did what he preferred. He did what was somehow right, provided it turned his stomach. His path of virtue was strewn with the wreckage of aircraft, the empty pails of kerosene, the charred fragments of glittering cabarets. A few syringes. And now—the corpse of a little girl. To some people, the enterprise—to find this Piper—might seem exemplary, even noble. But to Lucas Jameson it meant getting up in the morning, looking himself in the mirror. Shaving.

Returning to his apartment one night, a week after meeting Louise Cole, Lucas realized that he was being followed. He had been to the grocery store and was carrying a bag of cat food and paper towels. The girl averted her face as he walked by. He had seen her earlier in the day. So he ducked into a cigarette store and dropped his groceries. He chased the girl down the street. She ran pretty fast, and it was a block before he caught up with her. He put a hand out, grasped her shoulder and turned her around, then pushed her into a brick wall.

"Lay off me." The girl put up her arms defensively. "I didn't do anything."

She was skimpy, with straw hair.

"You've been following me," he said. And he imagined that, far away in Washington State, his mother was somehow experiencing this moment with him. *Now you finally know what I mean, Lucas.*

"I was—" She didn't deny it.

"Why?"

"I just wanted to get a look at you."

"What for?"

"Let me go." She was near tears. He relaxed his grip. They were on Eighth Street. A few tourists had stopped to watch. The girl was dressed in tight pants and purple gym shoes. She looked like a prostitute. She was reaching into her glittering bag. "Here."

Into his hand she thrust an envelope. "What's this?"

"Open it."

He began to walk and cut the envelope with his thumbnail. She dropped in by his side. He stopped beneath a street lamp.

Am sending Phyllis Lantern—
for fishing in the dark.

He read the old woman's scrawl and looked up. "You know what this is about?"

She nodded. "You hurt my head. I just wanted to see you first."

He tore the note into little shreds. "Let's not stand around," he said. "I left my groceries across the street."

They returned to his apartment and he made her coffee because, as she said:

"I love coffee."

"How long have you been drinking it?"

"Since I was seven."

"How old are you now?"

"Fourteen."

Phyllis Lantern would be pretty in a couple of years, if she lived that long. She had light blue eyes and high cheekbones where the baby flesh was still melting away. She was small-boned, and wore jeans and a yellow turtleneck sweater. She sat cross-legged on the couch in the living room, smoking a cigarette. He poured her coffee, sank into the ragged club chair, and asked:

"Are you a runaway?"

"No." She spooned more sugar into her espresso, which he had made extra bitter. "I came to New York about two weeks ago. I hitched a ride with a priest." She sipped her coffee and sat back. "He was a communist."

"Communist priests are very chic," nodded Lucas.

"He was gay."

"That's even better. Gay communist priests are the cream of the crop."

"Hasn't it always been true?"

"Commie gay—"

"Just gay," said Phyllis. "Karl Marx—"

"Wasn't gay."

"Or a priest. But I read he had carbuncles."

Lucas smiled, not at the bad joke but in admiration of the old woman, Louise Cole. He never would have found a girl like this by himself. She looked young enough and seemed canny, and if it was true that she wasn't a runaway, there wasn't the risk of righteous parents. He hadn't considered before what a rare specimen was required.

"I come from Davenport," she was saying. "And Rock Island, and Bettendorf, Moline,"

Lucas counted his fingers. "The Quad Cities."

"Except the fourth is East Moline, and I lived in all of them," said Phyllis. "One time or another."

"Why New York?"

"My father died." Phyllis crushed her cigarette in the glass ashtray and drew a cross in the ashes. "It was about a year ago. He played the drums. Maybe you heard of him. Glenn Miller was already dead. I was all ready to go to high school. We never had any money. Music is a dying profession, he used to say. It was last spring—"

"What was his name?"

"Jesse Lantern." Phyllis picked up her coffee and spilled some on the rug. "That was how I found Louise. Musicians have a way—"

"What about your mother?"

"Hey!" Phyllis put her coffee cup trembling into the saucer. "This is the third degree."

Lucas nodded.

"I guess I could've gone back there," sighed Phyllis. She cupped her chin in her palm and looked away. "Tennessee, near Morgan Spring. Jesse took me away from her when I was five. Because of the lice in my hair."

"Lice?" Lucas leaned forward. "Head lice?"

"My mother is a mountain woman," nodded Phyllis. "Jesse, I mean my father, was from Louisville and he'd been in the Army. They make you wash there, he said. After they were divorced he came to see me every weekend and washed the lice out of my scalp. Finally he just took me."

"My mother didn't have lice," said Lucas. "She had hallucinations."

"What kind?"

He shrugged. "It was the fifties. Rockefeller was one of them, beaming radio messages from the Empire—never mind." He stood up suddenly. "Do you want a drink?"

"I don't drink. I don't even smoke pot. It's a chemical age, but that doesn't make it good, you know."

"That's very refreshing," said Lucas. He got himself a glass and poured a brandy.

"So, after Jesse died, I started fucking," continued Phyllis. She lit another cigarette and her fingers were trembling. "I used to dance, too, at this little bar in Bettendorf until the police wouldn't let me. They called me an exhibitionist. But it doesn't matter what people call you, does it? There were a whole lot of train engineers in Rock Island, too. Once I fucked a real old guy. He had kind of yellow skin just as smooth as silk—" She looked up suddenly, and watched him pour a second brandy. "Are you a drunk?"

"No." Lucas drank.

"My father was," said Phyllis. "I used to hide his bottles."

Lucas felt the brandy warm him. "I bet you were good at it, too."

"Whiskey killed him, actually."

"It's killed many a man."

"It has." She smiled at him bravely. "And after I started fucking I had to have money, so I started hooking. I could make a lot of money that way. It kills something inside you. After a while the police picked me up. Three of them fucked me and one was a sergeant."

"That's when—"

"I left Bettendorf then," Phyllis nodded. "If you start letting the pigs fuck you, where will it all end?"

"Youth wants to know," said Lucas.

"You got it," nodded Phyllis resolutely. She narrowed her eyes. "You're not a cop, are you?"

"No."

"I knew you weren't—"

"What did Louise tell you?" he asked suddenly.

She gave him a look of *Why did you want to ask that?* "About—she called it—white slavery?"

"What did she say?"

"She kind of said—"

Lucas opened his palms and looked at them. His life line was rather short. But they could send him away for however long it lasted. He should have thought of that before. *You should have given that due weight, Mr. Jameson.* Sound of gavel. She was saying:

"Look, I'll help you out, okay? I don't care what it is. I need a place to stay. The cops pick me up all the time on Tenth Avenue and it isn't fair. I'll help you, I'll—"

"*What did the old lady say—*"

As he shouted, she was trying to light a cigarette with the butt of another, but her hands were shaking. He tossed her the matches and she fumbled with them. When he repeated himself, vexing her, she broke her cigarette and, hurling it and matches to the floor, screamed at him:

"*She told me you were a pimp!*"

Lucas stared coldly.

"*She said I was the bait and you were the pimp and going to sell me and maybe I would die! You're a pimp—a fucking pimp!*"

She had to hurry to keep up with him. He had fled the apartment. He crossed Astor Place and headed up Third Avenue. She had worked Third Avenue one night, across from the Variety Photoplays. It was not much money and it was cold. Tonight, though, was balmy. The warm air was soft and skimmed. Clouds hung clear of half a moon.

"I didn't mean it like that, Lucas. Louise said *like* a pimp, but not really."

He didn't answer.

"Lucas. What are you thinking about?"

"License plates."

"*Lucas—*"

His Christian name. He couldn't believe her—and yet there was no question but what he would do it.

He only needed a little air. Louise Cole had sent him a slightly tarnished gem. An orphan, a budding adolescent—manna from the heavenly thighs. He would go through hell putting her through hell. He would be a fool not to, a coward and a—

"If you're afraid I'm going to get you in trouble—"

"I'm not," he said abruptly.

"You say yourself—"

"Say what?"

He lost her for a second and stopped. Turning back, she had dug into her bag and brought out a book. She was rifling the pages and walking toward him. *A Flame for Charlie* . . .

"Listen here: *Every question of risk has been undermined in a society which has as its greatest passion—*"

He picked the book out of her hands, ripped it down the spine and tossed it onto Third Avenue.

"Lucas—that's my book!"

At Ninth Street Lucas lurched onto the old Triangle, where ancient houses oppressed the neighborhood with sturdy brick and solid foundations. He didn't know where he was going. But at St. Marks in the Bowery he halted.

"It's a church," said Phyllis. "I hate them."

"It burned down."

"Good."

They had rebuilt it. Lucas squeezed through the iron gate and went around the chapel yard. If recollec-

tion served, Peter Stuyvesant was buried here somewhere. The Dutchman with a wooden leg had married a twelve-year-old. *Way to go, Peter. You should
have given that due weight, Mr. Stuyvesant.*

"Why did you want to come *here*?"

He mounted the steps to Parish Hall. The big door
was locked.

"You don't believe in God," Phyllis said firmly.

Lucas sighed. "No." He turned and sat down
abruptly on the steps. He mumbled, "They used to
have poetry readings sometimes. I thought—"

"It's almost midnight," said Phyllis.

She sat down beside him.

He remembered, in fact, when Parish Hall was
crummy and dingy and filled with scraggly anarchists
boostering Ho Chi Minh. Speed freaks like autumn
leaves.

"What's the matter, Lucas?"

For the first time he felt her warmth, as she sat
beside him, like some kind of bird. She must have
weighed seventy-nine pounds. She pulled her hair
back, so he could see her face.

"Louise told me you weren't ever married," said
Phyllis. "But, I mean, you *do* like girls—"

"Women," he said.

Phyllis smiled. "A girl is just a little woman."

"Not in the eyes of—" He shook his head at that
old saw. "It depends on your perspective."

"Right," nodded Phyllis. "Like these freaks who
want to fuck twelve-year-olds. They *really* want six-
year-olds. You can't ever get exactly—"

"No," said Lucas. "You're right."

Although he had never been married, Lucas had
two ex-fiancées. One was at Austen Riggs, the men-

tal hospital in Stockbridge, Massachusetts. It was her second home. The other was a journalist permanently assigned to North Korea. Lucas thought—had been reflecting just the other day—that their combined emotional age was probably about six years old.

"I just assumed that we'd ball," said Phyllis. "But we don't have to if you don't want. We can be like brother and sister, until these—what do you call them?"

"White slavers," said Lucas.

"Yeah. Until they come get me."

He had long been drawn to such women. It perplexed him. But their inner worlds—mostly wilderness, with the bleached bones of ex-husbands here and there—fascinated him in ways he could not explain.

"I mean, we're not going to fall in love or anything," said Phyllis. She lit a cigarette and inhaled deeply—as deeply, he thought, as her tiny lungs would allow.

"No, not love," he said.

Which had not concerned him until now. It seemed to Lucas that a prerequisite to love was sanity, and the women to which he was led were just not that way. They were lunatics, and not just those among them who found their way into hospital.

"Besides," said Phyllis, "Louise said that when it was all over, if I was alive, you were going to help me."

"I was—"

"She told me to tell you. You're supposed to send me to school. Kind of as in payment."

"Really?"

Phyllis wasn't crazy, though. She needed a job. She wanted to go to school, too. He could see that.

She was going to ruin his life if he didn't wreck hers first, and both of them would regret this. But maybe not. A skeptical sense of hope, of invulnerability, spread within him like a toxin.

"Finishing school," said Phyllis.

"Finis—"

"Some school she went to in Chicago, I don't know."

And when this time she leaned into him, he put an ancient arm around her. She let her head fall towards his chest. She wore whatever perfume they always used. Her jaw had a hard angle, and there was a dark bruise on her throat. These perforations in decorum didn't bother him. Decorum was not his strongest point.

"Mrs. Wellsey's," he remembered.

"I'd rather go to, like, Cal Tech."

Lucas nodded. When he kissed her, he heard a wooden leg knocking. A sigh in the churchyard, her heart the gavel and—and Stuyvesant had company.

SIX

At 5:29 Quinta Mechanic turned over in bed one minute before the alarm went off. She always beat that clock. She rubbed her eyes and yawned. It was still dark outside. The night had been cool and the bedroom window was open a crack. Quinta reached across her husband and closed it. She patted his belly and, without a word, got out of bed and trundled naked into the bathroom.

She washed her face and brushed her teeth, then pulled down an old sweatshirt and a pair of levis that were hanging from the bathroom door. She picked up a pair of anklets and sneakers in the bedroom, where she heard her husband just beginning to wake. In the kitchen she drank a glass of orange juice on her way out the door. She started to jog once she reached the lobby.

Jogging was so fashionable these days that, even so early in the morning, Central Park South was punctuated with executives in sweatsuits. Quinta didn't think much of these men, nor did she much care to run with them. Probably because they were afraid of a lingering thief in the park, some of them only ran along its perimeter. Quinta couldn't imagine anyone mugging her, so she crossed the street and ran along the old stone wall to the Plaza Hotel, rounded the statue of General Sherman, and jogged languidly into Central Park. She had a course that she followed every morning. It was three miles long.

There were two reasons that Quinta ran every morning that rain or snow didn't put her on the jogging pad in the bedroom. Physique was one. Quinta simply found that the extra hundred calories she burned were enough to keep her weight at a trim two hundred pounds. She was a big woman, 5' 10", and big-boned with thick shoulders and broad hips. Although her belly was not flat, she was by no means overweight, and at the age of thirty-nine, very little if any part of her sagged. Her arms were nine inches at the biceps, and her thighs were thick and muscular. She had a big bosom, but her breasts were still proud, and when her husband made love to her, he liked to leave the lights burning. She had a full face with a high, straight brow and dark eyes. Her nose was long and flared, though slightly crooked from once being broken. Her lips were thin and determined. Quinta was not pretty in the usual sense, but her short black hair framed curiously attractive features.

The other reason that Quinta Mechanic ran every morning was that she had been doing it for twenty-five years, and saw no reason not to continue. She no longer lifted weights or worked out at the gym, apart from a hundred laps in the pool three times a week. Jogging had been just a part of her training, and although Quinta rankled at much of her past, she could not deny that her body was part of the parcel she always would be. She was only grateful that she had got to her head before it was too late.

Every morning along the lake, near the weeping willows and the flowering cherry trees, Quinta met the old man running the other way. He looked about sixty and all she knew about him was that he lived at the Sherry-Netherland. She raised her hand.

"How's tricks?"

"Lousy."

They always were for him. Quinta picked up a little natural speed going downhill. It had rained the day before and the pavement was still wet and a bit soft.

In her twenties Quinta had been a lady wrestler. It was a natural occupation for her, not just because she was big but because she was the daughter of Ironsides Jackson. She had grown up wrestling with him and his friends on the living room floor, where Ironsides had laid down a regulation mat. She had started getting interested at about age twelve and had begun training in earnest when she was fourteen. At twenty she had her first professional match with a hair-pulling ripsnorter named Bertha Steel, and lost because she was supposed to. But soon after that she started calling herself Quinta Mechanic and got in some good matches as the better half of a tag team with Limehouse Wilma.

It was also natural that Quinta's first marriage, when she was twenty-two, was to Warhorse Durant from Buffalo. He was three hundred pounds of savage muscle and nobody dared ask him whether he could read or write. Except Quinta, who knew how to get out of his hammerlocks. He was an animal in bed, and shortly after Quinta began to think there might be more to sex than ten vicious thrusts *a tergo* and then good-night, she divorced him. She also ended her wrestling career, with a terrifying double scissors and airplane spin assault on Lilac Lilly Masters, all against the script, at the Stockyards in Chicago.

Quinta moved back to New York in the late 1960s, but she didn't return to Brighton Beach, which had been her childhood home and was where her father still roamed the boardwalk after his morning workout. Instead, she moved to Manhattan and started to do what was, for her, an unusual thing. Day and night, in a studio on Crosby Street in the district later known as Soho, Quinta Mechanic began to paint.

At first she did simple things—the trees and flowers and houses that filled the learn-to-draw books she bought and studied diligently. But when she started to take art courses, first at Stuyvesant and later at the New School, she turned to abstract expressionism. Quinta was built to work like Jackson Pollock, perhaps even more than Pollock was, and she looked much the enraged paintress when she stood astride her canvases stretched on the floor, paint dripping from her hands and arms.

It was a couple of years before she gathered the courage to show her paintings to anyone, and she didn't know how to go about it. But Merrill Robbins had a gallery on 57th Street, and more by chance than design, she took her paintings there. Merrill, a small, slender man who was proper and, at his best, ironic, took a good look at her work. He nodded thoughtfully at each canvas, then pursed his lips and smiled at her. Eventually he adjusted his tie and said, just a little nervously:

"You can't paint."

That took some courage, even if Merrill didn't know it. Quinta knew the rage of rejection, and for a moment she considered making of Merrill Galleries a whole new kind of show.

"However," said Merrill, as he adjusted his glasses and smiled, "what about a little dinner?"

She agreed, still smarting. But it went quite well. Merrill listened to her, fascinated, and he responded with ease and charm over prime ribs and red wine at Sardi's. Then he gave her a book on German art since the war and another one on Marcel Duchamp.

"What I mean to say," he told her, "is that perhaps you don't need to paint to be an artist."

So Quinta Mechanic had become an artist, in fact, though not one who painted or held any exhibitions. Her work was incomplete but growing. She didn't get written up in the art journals, and wouldn't have liked to be. Occasionally, however, some of what she did showed up in the newspapers, but it was anonymous. If she were an artist, though, it didn't really matter, did it? No, she was confident, it didn't.

Quinta Mechanic emerged from Central Park on the Columbus Circle side. It was nearing six in the morning and the sun was brightening the sky. Quinta trotted across 59th Street and into the apartment house at 230 Central Park South. Merrill Robbins would be up now, in the kitchen preparing his breakfast. He was her second marriage; it was working.

Merrill left early for the gallery that morning, and Quinta spent an hour dusting and tidying up the living room. She had an appointment, due at nine o'clock.

The living room, which overlooked the park, was warm, not too big, and well appointed but not overdone. Two wingback chairs flanked the fireplace, opposite a long comfortable divan. There were four Sheridan chairs around a square walnut table, and that was where she planned to seat her guest. He would be able to gaze up at her favorite painting, the untitled Pollock that hung over the mantel. If he turned toward the window, he could also see one of the signed copies of Duchamp's Green Box, with the ninety-three documents for *The Bride Stripped Bare* spilled across a marble chess table. It was one of twenty deluxe copies that included a manuscript page, and when Merrill had presented it to Quinta on their first anniversary, it was worth a small fortune.

A little before nine, after changing out of her housecoat into her usual outfit—parachute pants dyed yellow and a red flannel shirt—Quinta went into the kitchen. From the refrigerator she removed a round gelatine mold and a small bowl of heavy whipped cream. She had made the jello the night before; now she ran a little hot water over the mold, and turned it onto a crystal serving plate.

It was double-tiered and had come out beautiful. She had made the peach flavor first and folded into the thickening jello a cup of fresh-cut strawberries. Separately, she had laced raspberry jello with both blueberries and apple slices, and when they were both just stiff enough, combined them. It was not difficult to make, though if the two jellos weren't united at precisely the right moment, they could run together. They hadn't.

Quinta brought the dessert plate into the living room and placed it in the middle of the big table; she set out spoons and napkins. Not long after she'd laid out two goblets and a silver pitcher, Quinta glanced at her watch. It was two minutes past nine. The doorbell rang.

The visitor at the door was a short, slender man dressed in a light brown polyester suit with a thin yellow tie hanging on a beige shirt. His face was bony and drawing uncomfortably into middle age; he had a small mouth and nose. His eyes were blue and set far apart. It was not a pleasant face, but Quinta had not expected one.

She offered her hand: "Quinta Mechanic."

He said, "My name is Jonathan."

She waved him in.

Jonathan Barnes stepped quickly inside. He removed his hat, a lemon fedora, which Quinta took without asking and tossed along the living room couch. He watched it go.

"We're over here."

When Jonathan pulled up to the big table, he

noticed the painting above the mantel. It was abstract and he didn't like it. He turned over a number of comments in his mind before saying nothing.

"The artist's wife gave that to me," said Quinta. "Lee Krassner. Do you know her work?"

"No." Jonathan stared. "I don't." He thought again about what to say that would be positive, and finally decided on, "It's very nice."

"Nice isn't the word," said Quinta.

No, probably not. But at his most sensitive moments Jonathan Barnes was not much of an art critic, and this morning his eye for beauty was even groggier than usual. He had just come from a brief chat with a woman from Scarsdale, New York, named Thelma Whitehall, over orange juice at Nedicks.

"There's jello," Quinta said. She sliced him a shivering wedge. "Whipped cream?"

Jonathan nodded. He didn't know whether he was hungry or not, but he wouldn't have refused. He took the plate she offered, waited ostensibly from courtesy until she made a plate for herself, and then had a first bite. It was good and he said so.

"Thank you," said Quinta. "I don't believe that a big breakfast is always the best thing."

"Neither do I," said Jonathan.

"Unless you have an active day ahead of you." Quinta poured herself a glass of carrot juice and offered him the pitcher. He declined. "I let my body tell me what kind of breakfast I need," said Quinta, "and then I let it know what I think."

Jonathan Barnes allowed the whipped cream to swirl at the roof of his mouth before swallowing it. He watched the woman across the table as she slivered a glistening piece of fruit onto her spoon and then dipped it in a little whipped cream. It looked good that way, and he did likewise.

"You come from the South, don't you?" asked Quinta. "I can tell just by the way you dress. Or am I wrong?"

"You're not wrong," said Jonathan.

"Not that I care," she added. "I wouldn't care if you were from the South Pole."

He tightened his lips to a smile. "My mother was born in Georgia. I never lived there, though."

"No. You don't sound Deep South."

"Mother does," he said. "Not always."

Quinta took her last bite of jello. "Like New York?"

Jonathan shrugged. "I don't love it."

She put her napkin up, laid her forearms on the table, and pushed away her plate. Lacing her fingers and leaving her thumbs to tangle for position she commented, "Yeah, well. Too many people love New York."

This man, thought Quinta, was a professional. She didn't know what profession or whether he was good at what he did, but he certainly was in business. Often the people who consigned Quinta work were not—and the more interesting among them would not even sit down. Fearful, they would pace her living room and ask how they could eat with this so-and-so gnawing at their stomachs, or else, angry, they would devour dessert and ask for more, and coffee, please. Quinta would often relieve their fear or rage just by being quiet; they would leave, confident, and Quinta would be inspired.

With professionals it was difficult. They had something they wanted her to accomplish, a deed of which they wanted to wash their hands. They sat quietly, like Jonathan Barnes, and said little. They provided plenty of money but little aesthetic gratification.

"I almost forgot," smiled Jonathan. He laid down his spoon and reached into an inside pocket. Across the table he laid an envelope.

Quinta waited a moment before folding the envelope three times and dropping it into her flapped shirt pocket.

"I'll give you this, too."

Jonathan shoved the matches toward her. The name was always given to her in the same way, by professionals and amateurs alike. Often torn, always printed in pencil. Once on a movie stub, another time on a gum wrapper. She was making a collection of them. This time the name was written on the inside of a matchbook cover, in which all the matches were burnt. Quinta dropped it into her pocket after glancing at the name.

"Do you work alone?" asked Jonathan. He finished his second helping, then pushed away his plate and put up his napkin.

"You see anybody else?"

"I just wondered."

A lot of people wondered, and the only reason for it, Quinta thought, was that she was a woman. Nobody wondered whether a hit *man* worked alone; hit *men* almost always did. It bothered her that women faced such handicaps, and she was just waiting for the day she met Phyllis Schlafly.

"You don't trust me," suggested Quinta.

"I didn't mean that," said Jonathan. "No."

He did trust her, in fact. Not only did she look like she could go twenty rounds with a Kodiak bear, but,

Jonathan suspected, Quinta could outthink and outwit Will and Ariel Durant. He poured himself some carrot juice and tried it. "It's just not the way I usually do business."

"Yeah," said Quinta. "You usually do business in telephone booths, right?"

"Not always." Jonathan sometimes did business in hotel rooms. However, it was true that if he had a nickel for every time he had stepped into a telephone booth, he certainly would have been a wealthy man.

"Well, not me." Quinta laced her hands around the back of her neck. She leaned back. "And there are two reasons for it."

"It's okay," said Jonathan. He didn't like the carrot juice, but guessed you could acquire a taste for it.

"Number one is that I think it's crude," said Quinta. "And number two, I don't consider this a business."

"What isn't a business?"

"Never mind." Quinta shook her head.

Lectures on art and aesthetics usually did not touch professionals, and that was certain to be true of the man sitting across from her. She couldn't communicate with someone who thought Jackson Pollock was "nice" and who didn't so much as glance at Marcel Duchamp tumbling the bride. There was no point in trying. The only thing she could do was to find out what it was that, for the five thousand dollars in an envelope in her shirt pocket, she was supposed to do to the man whose name was on the matchbook cover. She would try to make it beautiful; she would do her best and try to be proud of it—that was all.

"Okay," she said, and raised her goblet to drink the last of her carrot juice. "Now, who in the hell is Lucas Jameson?"

SEVEN

Lucas waked that morning to Persistence ringing the doorbell. His room, windowless, was dark, and when he turned the clock, it glowed eleven-thirty. He could not immediately leave the bed, perhaps because it was warmer than usual. Because of the girl. The sleeping form beside him stirred, and when he touched it and felt the hard curve of her shoulder within the crook of his arm, a wave of bittersweet emotion swept over him. He shivered. The doorbell rang again.

He put his feet on the floor and looked back at the girl. Experimentally he touched her, and her thin lips involuntarily grimaced, then extended to a smile, and finally lapsed into their original pout. The room was warm and musty. He lifted the covers almost curiously—yes, quite curiously. She lay on her side, facing him, naked. For a moment he regarded her body—skinny and small-breasted, with pointed nipples, and more than a hint of oncoming womanhood. In all, there was an economy of lines to her body that lent him the brief, ridiculous idea that he had slept with a drawing by Picasso. He stood up and slipped into slacks. Catching a glimpse of himself in the mirror, he told himself with some glimmer of satisfaction that his own body was, indeed, almost hairless and that the guilty-looking uncircumcised member was, after all, not too long or thick.

But as he moved to answer the door, he caught her scent on his fingers as he picked up a cigarette; then the night, which had just ended, returned to him, in its shuddering simplicity. He trembled.

The woman was leaning on the bell by the time he opened the door. Dressed in a two-piece camel-hair suit with a pink scarf billowing at her neck, she had on ruby lipstick, slightly smeared. She wasn't smiling. Her eyes were dark and strident. Joan Crawford was dead. It had to be Thelma Whitehall.

"Lucas, my God."

He turned away. She followed him inside and let the door slam behind her. It set his head throbbing. The brandy.

"You look like absolute hell."

"My body is—never mind."

Lucas padded barefoot into the kitchen and broke apart the espresso pot. His head felt quite large from what had seemed to him a really unremarkable amount of brandy. He watched the coffee grounds disappear in little clumps down the drain. Drinks, which he evidently had needed to break the domination of the social conventions that somehow proscribed an older and a younger, an April and November, from . . . but two *people* is what they were, after all. He ruminated with a hangover.

Thelma Whitehall touched his naked back. "For Christ's sake, look at your—"

"Enough." She was exaggerating. There might have been a scratch on his back; the girl had been excited. Lucas reached for the coffee can. "What's new, Thelma?"

"Not much. Read about your getting shot. Any scars?"

"None visible." Not even his shoulders were tight any more.

"Did you like the tangerines?"

"Not much," he admitted. He had given the basket of fruit to the nurses at St. Vincent's. The sisters had gathered around and each picked her favorite. "Was it you?"

"No." Thelma rummaged in her bag for a cigarette. "It was Sarah Trilling. You know I wouldn't send you a basket of fruit. *Bon voyage* and all that."

"I thought it was a little hostile."

"Sarah's very grateful to you, actually. If you'd mentioned her name, it would have ruined her marriage."

Lucas set the flame high. "I thought she hated him."

"You know what I mean."

He didn't really.

"It would've halved her alimony."

Lucas nodded. "Yeah."

Thelma pulled up to the kitchen table and sat down smoking. She offered him another cigarette and he took it. It was a purple Vogue cigarette by Nat Sherman. He lighted it with the flame from the stove.

"As for me," said Thelma, "I'm bored."

That was not news. Thelma Whitehall had a husband who made $150,000 a year, two children, a twelve-room house with cut crystal chandeliers, and a private bath with a bidet. She was bored. She was tired of cheating on her husband, worn out from child-rearing, and no longer cared about telling the maids to wash the ceilings. She was thirty-five years old.

Despite all that, for Lucas, she had been an excellent source of information. Thelma knew every arm in Westchester County. She had known the doctors who prescribed everything from Valium to Percodan, and the pharmacies that filled them, and even the treasury agents who were bribed to look the other way. When nobody else would talk to Lucas, Thelma had called him every day and talked for hours. Not without recompense, of course, and Lucas had to contribute a little morphine on his own. When he had started to take it himself, Thelma was warmly encouraging. At the time it seemed only a natural extension of getting the story. Few people can become addicts even if they try. Lucas had been surprised when he turned out to be one of them.

Lucas leaned against the stove and smoked. "What brings you to Manhattan this—"

"Rainy morning," said Thelma. "My husband's in Chicago, the kids are in school, and the goddamn maids are out to lunch. Where else would I be?"

Lucas shrugged.

"Actually," she continued, "a wonderful thing happened to me this morning. Marvelous in fact."

Lucas shut his eyes and rubbed them with the heels of his hands. A wonderful thing for Thelma would be a new set of arms. Marvelous would be a hot line to a poppy field.

"This is a once-in-your-lifetime," she said.

"What is?"

Thelma went into her cavernous bag. Not the lipstick, powder puff, hair spray, rabbit's foot, nasal mist or diaphragm. A bottle.

"Dristan?"

"Look inside," she urged.

He pried off the cap and spread some pills in his hand.

"Forty of them," said Thelma proudly. "What do I need with Erma Brombeck?"

"You need William Burroughs," said Lucas.

They were Dilaudid. Yellows with the number 4 stamped on each one, which meant four milligrams— which signified, in turn, for Thelma, a sum of ecstasy.

"How much, Lucas? Guess."

Lucas fed the tablets back into the bottle. "I don't know."

"Fifty bucks."

Cheap.

"It's unbelievable, Lucas. This is a *very reliable* connection, too."

Any question hereafter would be rhetorical, he thought. Lucas crossed his arms and watched her. Thelma removed her wristwatch, then took off her suit jacket and tucked it around the back of her chair. She unbuttoned her blouse and took it off. She was wearing a black brassiere. Her figure was good. Her arms weren't so good. Lucas sighed.

"Do you have a saucepan?"

Lucas turned to the stove as the coffee pot erupted. He turned it over to drip and burned his thumb. While he sucked on it, Thelma found a saucepan herself and put up a little water. She had her own eye dropper. She always carried one in her change purse. Lucas heard his name called, weakly.

"Hi."

Phyllis—in the doorway. She was wrapped in a bedsheet, eyes slitted, face pale and soft. Altogether youthful. Lucas smiled good morning.

"Hello there," said Thelma. She was fingering a brassiere strap while watching her water boil. To Lucas she added, "Introduce me?"

Phyllis stared. "I didn't mean to—"

"That's okay," said Lucas. "This is Thelma."

"I should put something on," said Phyllis.

"Not on my account." Thelma shook her head.

Phyllis lifted the bedsheet so she could walk. She disappeared.

"Lucas," said Thelma. She lifted the spoon and the dropper from the water and reattached the bulb. "Isn't she a little *young*?"

"She's a Soviet astronaut."

"She's hardly out of—"

"She's old enough," snapped Lucas. He brought down a cup and saucer and waited impatiently for the coffee to finish. Did he run a youth hostel or a shooting gallery? He didn't know. But who was Thelma Whitehall to come to his apartment at noon to cook junk and what did she know from bobby sox? Why had she come anyway? He didn't need it. He poured himself a cup of thick black coffee. It occurred to him then—

"You have any points?" Thelma was coaxing a pill from the bottle onto the spoon.

The coffee was scalding. "Points?"

It was an interesting question. Not so long ago Lucas had four dozen monoject syringes, five-eighths of an inch long, sitting in his bedroom closet in a couple of cigar boxes. Of course, he had thrown them all away. All but one.

"I'll get it," he said.

"You're a doll," said Thelma.

In the bathroom Phyllis was washing her face. Lucas helped her to dry it. He lifted her onto the sink and she wrapped her legs around his hips. As they kissed, and her mouth was fresh and cool, he reached into the medicine chest. The point was nestled innocently in the box of foot powder. He disentangled himself.

"Stay here."

She sensed the alarm in his voice. "What's wrong?"

"Just a friend of mine with a problem," said Lucas. "Take a bath."

Phyllis looked doubtfully into the tub. "Wasn't this what happened to—"

"That was in the hall," said Lucas.

"Who is—"

He ducked out abruptly. When he got back to the kitchen, Thelma had her solution all prepared. Lucas tossed the syringe on the table. The woman smiled warmly, her lips wet. She reached up and put a hand on his cheek in a way he didn't like, saying:

"We'll each take half."

He nodded. "Sure."

"Once won't hurt, darling."

"No."

"Of course, there's more where this came from."

"You always say that."

Thelma shrugged. "I do, don't I?" She acted as though in a trance, gazed at the syringe as if it were a baby. He picked it out of her hands. That was what she wanted. He said:

"I'll do it to you."

"Thanks," said Thelma quietly.

Lucas drew the belt off his slacks and handed it to her. Thelma wrapped it tight above her elbow. He sat down and pulled his chair close, then locked one of his legs between both of hers. When Thelma lay forth her arm, he searched for the vein. It was hard to find.

"This is going to be wonderful," she said.

"Amazing." He slowly massaged the abused flesh.

"That it's—"

"That it's still there."

Thelma bit her lip. "You're a fuck, Lucas."

He found where the vein was hiding. He moved even closer and held her firmly. He pumped her arm until the vein rose a bit. When he inserted the needle, her face remained impassive. He drew some blood into the syringe.

"You always were good at this," said Thelma, with all sincerity and thanks. "You always could."

Lucas smiled vaguely. He went back into the vein with the dope, then drew it up again, mixed it with the blood, the way she always liked, until her eyes were lightly closed, lids fluttering, and she was beginning to think about space breasts, ocean brine on tap, amoeba dolls. With his free hand Lucas unstrapped the belt and it dropped to the floor.

"Now," said Thelma.

Lucas left the needle full.

"Now!"

There were moments in life when it was very lucky to have had a paranoid mother. Paranoids are suspicious people who notice little things; paranoid mothers convey this capacity to their offspring. Lucas Jameson felt very lucky. He left the needle full.

"Please? Lucas?"

He took her chin between thumb and forefinger. "You must be bored."

She was afraid. *"For Christ's sake, Lucas—"*

"Why don't you go corrupt some nice young boy, Thelma? Some high school flop-eared kid who plays football? You could have him after practice. I don't have any cookies, Jimmy, but there's this milk in a warhead—"

"Lucas—"

"Why me?"

"You're my—"

"I'm your friend, Thelma."

When she started to cry, in short bursts of tears, he felt sorry for her. If he just filled her up with that fluid, she would be fine. Several times she tried to jerk her arm free, but he held it tight. The needle got testy in her arm and must have hurt. Finally, he asked her:

"Who was it?"

Thelma breathed between sobs. "This little man."

"Who?"

"I don't know him; he gave me the forty."

"If you came to see me."

She gazed at him sidelong with scared eyes. "I was going to tell you, Lucas."

"His name?"

Her lipstick was running, and her tongue was out of her mouth. "Jonathan—"

"Last name?"

"No—"

He shrugged. No last names in dopedom. They were coming after him. Like Gatling had said. That was the important thing. Jonathan was coming after him.

"I would've told you, Lucas. Honestly."

"Yes, Thelma. You did right."

"Now, Lucas?"

"Now."

He gripped her arm and shot her up.

EIGHT

Within seventy-two hours of Thelma Whitehall's visit Lucas abandoned his apartment. He took a room in the old Hotel Times Square on 43rd Street and Eighth Avenue. Once there had been muzak in every room. No longer. Phyllis left her nest at Louise Cole's boarding house to join him. She was young enough to have good manners and they shared a sweet tooth, but it was also peculiar. The day she first moved in coincided with her monthly cycle, and the first thing Lucas had to do was buy a box of junior-sized tampons at the unfashionable delicatessen where the Greek clerk liked to chase derelicts with a baseball bat. Phyllis emerged from the bathroom smiling.

"I'm a woman now," she joked.

Their room was on the fourteenth floor and overlooked 42nd Street. As the afternoon faded, the lights came up on the streamers of sex and violence. The Empire Theater was showing hammer murder movies; it cast off the dusky light from a neglected Romanesque facade. Next door was the entrance to Peepland where the red pupil in the neon eye, watching through a keyhole, blinked.

"Is that what you're going to do?" she asked him. "Look through keyholes?"

"Transom peepers, they used to be called," he smiled. "I'll try to stir up some interest."

"In me?"

"Yes."

"What will I do?" she asked cautiously.

He glanced from the window. "I should probably keep you on ice," he said. "Perfect and virginal."

"It's too late. What do you call it? White slavery?"

"It has a nice ring," he nodded.

"It's all right if you bring them up," she told him. "But no couples, and I don't like being watched."

She held this vague misapprehension that he was simply to act as her pimp. It was a wish. A pimp meant protection, beyond which the boundaries of sex for hire and the business of buying and selling bodies wholesale became indistinguishable. The sex world had a prismatic quality. Light into its darker corners was readily deflected. She settled into one of them now, and lit a cigarette. Lucas stared at her, feeling a burst of moral rectitude settle to ashes within. He broke into a grin.

"That won't be necessary," he said. "Not right away."

"I mean, I don't mind being watched, but not while I'm fucking."

"It won't—"

"I'm not going to sit around here, anyway," she said. "I'll get a job."

"A job where?"

"Somewhere."

"You're too young."

"Get me some I.D."

"I don't—" He started to protest, from a profusion of competing motives. It was inarticulate.

"Forget it, Lucas." Phyllis offered him the cigarette, but he declined. She reached forward and patted his knee maternally. "The girl wants to work."

The dynamics of ecstasy—Lucas wrote later—*are obscure. On Times Square in New York they are especially perplexing, from the plastic Christ beside the marble dildo in the shop window to the efficient private booths for watching women on public display. But ecstasy persists: naked or clothed in leather, barefoot or in spike heels, black or white or in all the shades of the Caribbean and some of the Orient. It lives in a woman's body or in some part of her body. It is shown on celluloid and alluded to in print. It can be crested on the hairless lip of the boy playing the videogame at Fantasyland, whose image dances beneath the baldpate that eyes him hungrily. Sometimes ecstasy is lost in all the endeavors to find it, and under a full moon it can be extinguished.*

Others know more about ecstasy than I do, but they are probably its slave and not its master. There are not many masters. Masters are rare, perhaps extinct. I stalked one anyway, with industry. It requires industry, and intensity, to find one—even to hear of one from somebody else.

The men who work on Times Square serve as cogs in the machine of ecstasy. They are ex-sailors—or army men or marines—and Times Square is another port of fabulous call and an interminable beachhead for their most enduring and banal fantasies. These men are, for the most part, urban primitives. The thrill of their lives is to have administered artificial resuscitation to some luckless victim of cardiac arrest—usually the oversexed patron of a distraught prostitute, who lay gasping for breath in a sea of sweat, semen, and blood. The victim invariably died; the words 'I knew he was gonna croak' formulate the emblem of some common experience which reverberates to the deepest layers of the mind. But on ecstasy these men are silent.

The bosses on Times Square, those who run the peep shows and sex clubs and skin parlors, are less familiar with the problem than even those men who work for them. They are the little mobsters and relatives of mobsters; they are the mafiettes. But they know things, and insofar as people are things, they know people. In particular, they know that knowledge is dangerous. They do not impart it.

That leaves only—on the lower rack of afflicted enchantment—the purchaser patrons of ecstasy. But these men are, for the most part, so deluded by the

distortions of their own wishes as to be also useless.
A class of them, the people who once were categori-
cally termed perverts and who gained nothing from
the liberalization of labels, afford a special interest. I
spent some nights seeking them. They are a pleasant,
often unhappy group who, desperately wanting to find
love in a shoe or a whip, know something about
ecstasy. They know as much as can be learned from
leather and polish.

The nature of ecstasy did not fall quickly into my
hands . . .

But he looked, as he said, with industry. His only
cover, as a narcotics addict with vague connections
to pornography and "film," was genially accepted.
He hardly ever had even to say it. Sometimes the
police questioned him, but he told them nothing. They
searched him. Once he was arrested and he called
Roscoe Gatling, who had him sprung without a further word. On the street he was transformed, in a few
weeks, from stranger to habitué. He worked extremely
quietly. He was in no hurry. Money was no problem.
He had a little and could look forward to more, of
course, when he . . . when he sold her.

One bright afternoon he walked over to the Venus
Lounge. Louise Cole received him. She gave him an
old circular from Mrs. Wellsey's School of Advancement for Young Ladies. It must have been thirty
years old. He put it in his pocket. They talked about
other things; then she said:

"I knew Phyllis would suit you, Mr. Jameson."

He searched her eyes, her expression, for any trace
of guilt. After all, she was somehow complicit.
She had sent the girl to him so that he could sell
her.

"It's a dangerous business," Louise admitted quietly, sipping a Remy. "They might kill her. You don't know what might happen."

He nodded.

"And she's a good girl, too, a smart girl. I thought you'd like that. Her daddy died, that was it. Her mama—"

"Lice."

"Yes, that's right." Louise smiled distantly. "She's good and it might make it worse on us when she gets killed or otherwise ruined. Ain't that right?"

"Yes," he agreed. "Much tougher."

"And you got in with her, didn't you? You're involved."

He nodded abruptly. "Yes." And it dawned on him. "You knew I would, didn't you?"

"With that girl, yes." Louise spoke to her drink. "She's white, but I met her twice, do you see? Just got to be careful, don't fall in love. Get you killed and her both."

Hemlock, he thought. "Don't worry," he said obscenely, cavalierly. "I haven't ever—"

The old lady cut him off with a throaty sigh. "But you don't live to my age without taking risks. Ain't nothin' to sitting here and talkin' about bait, but then you got to go out and fish."

He didn't reply. Before he left, she mounted the little stage in the back and sat down before the piano. She played and sang *Shave 'Em Dry*:

> *I ain't gonna stand no quittin'*
> *Or no jumpin' down*
> *Before I let you quit me*

I'll burn Chicago down—
Baby, let me holler
Daddy's gotta shave 'em dry!

There were twenty verses to that, too.

NINE

It went on through April and part of May. The warm
weather upon them, they left the window open at
night to the ticking of the streets. Phyllis took a job
dancing at the Roxy burlesque house. Her stage name
was Caldonia. The Roxy was one of the few such
places left in New York, an intimate and tomb-like
theater above a Cantonese restaurant. The real names
of the live sex team, Tristan and Isolde, were Joe and

Maureen Scheckley. The other dancers, besides Phyllis, were Margot and Zelda. Margot was a lovely-toned Nigerian with tribal scars on her cheeks. She was narcoleptic and had to be roused from sleep before every performance. Zelda, who doubled as stage manager, was a statuesque redhead in her early forties and had worked the striptease circuit when it was real. She liked Phyllis and kept her off stage when the police were watching. Striptease, thought Zelda, was a dead art.

"And you'd better get out of it," she advised Phyllis, "before it's too late."

"I was planning on it," agreed Phyllis.

Lucas's search for the Piper baffled Phyllis. It was like participating in somebody's fairy tale. She had heard of the Piper as street talk, but he seemed no more real than Captain Hook. Lucas called it an anachronism, but he kept saying that anachronisms exist.

Phyllis worked at the burlesque house weekdays and Friday and Saturday nights. At the end of every day she asked Lucas:

"What's new on the Piper?"

And for a long time he always replied, "Nothing." He carried a small leather notebook, though, and often wrote in it. Phyllis was curious but never pried, even when it lay on the night table as he slept.

In April, too, Phyllis marked the anniversary of her father's death. It was another reason she was glad to be working. She didn't like to remember his final illness, the alcohol sickness, the Veterans' hospital, his jaundiced hands, the tremens, and the final, orphanizing telephone call at three in the morning. There was no phone in the room of the cheap hotel where they had been living, and she took the call in the lobby where, literally, mice lived in the old grandfather clock next to the vending machines. The night clerk had no sympathy.

But Jesse Lantern, in memory, was something else. He had often played the drums in burlesque shows. His girl friends had been showgirls. It was eerie, but somehow comforting, to imagine her father with the sticks, in the shadows of the stage, as she danced. In her mind she could still hear the backbeat that he supplied to the syrupy songs they played, as she lay on her back and scissored her legs. She undressed to two songs and danced completely naked to a third. Into a garter she slipped the dollar bills that men tossed on stage. For a dollar she would spread the lips of her cunt.

When Phyllis had first started dancing in a dark little tavern in Bettendorf, it had seemed easy, fun, artless and exciting. She even used to dance on her nights off. Jesse Lantern had been sick already and it helped pay expenses. But soon it had become her job, and then it was no longer fun. In New York it was always work.

Even if Jesse Lantern disapproved of the way strippers today took everything off, Phyllis knew that he would have preferred it for her over turning tricks. He would have hated to see her in the weeks and months after he died, just past her thirteenth birthday. She'd lost weight and color; her eyes changed. On the streets of Rock Island the nervous blonde in the tanktop with no bra and no belt on low-slung jeans— much the troubled exhibitionist—had been her. She dissolved endless Anacin into Tab for breakfast and grew to depend on Tussirex, a brand of cough syrup which was loaded with enough codeine to send a rocket to the moon. She retired into the shadows as the police cruised by.

"You keep me off the streets," she joked, now, with Lucas.

"You speak too soon," he replied.

What was with Lucas, anyway? She didn't know whether to love or hate him. He wasn't phony like a pimp, and he didn't take her money and stuff it in his shoe. He didn't tell her he loved her, either. Nor was he like a boyfriend, which she didn't want in any case. Yet she often thought about him and felt neglected when he sat in a corner and wrote in his notebook. She knew, too, that he liked her, and it made her nervous. Sometimes she just wished she could go to finishing school, like Louise wanted her to, and forget about men.

When she danced, Phyllis could see herself in the mirror. With her back to the audience she bent over and ran her hands along her thighs. In the mirror she saw herself naked and exposed, and wondered, as Lucas Jameson sometimes said that he, too, wondered: *Who is coming after you? Where are you going? Where are they taking you?*

In the early evenings Phyllis liked to sit with him at the window and watch the lights. It was best when they made love then, too—in the fresh night, when the excitement on the street below was at a pitch. After the first time, when she hadn't been able to count her orgasms, it took longer and longer and sometimes never happened at all. The weather turned from warm to almost hot.

In the half-light they lay naked on the bed and he

worked on her. Her eyes were closed and her heart pounded. He was beside her, or went down on her. The old wooden muzak box was still on the wall but produced no sound. His orgasms were more intense if they made love a second time, but he said they also made him feel guilty. Once they climaxed at about the same moment, while she lay turned on her side toward the open window where the curtains rode on the breeze. He was inside her from behind, with his hand on her lower belly and one finger on her clitoris. When it was over, she couldn't help herself and turned around and wept in his arms.

They didn't like to be seen together, but that night they had dinner at Childs. Not many people ate there because it was so tawdry yet expensive. Before going they took a shower together. At the restaurant she sat across from him without makeup or lipstick, in a clean halter top and white pants creased from the dry cleaner. He himself had not shaved for a month, and his beard had assumed its scraggly dark finish. Over coffee he lit a cigarette and said:

"I'm getting close."

TEN

It was a rough Irish bar on 39th Street. Freud was dead. Havelock Ellis, dead. Alfred Kinsey, dead ninety-five percent. Masters and Johnson were in St. Louis. But Gus Sagze was still in his late twenties, gangling and awkward. He wore a polyester leisure suit with big flapped pockets. Thick glasses on his face slid down his nose, above a wide mouth with thin lips. Lucas sat beside him and ordered them both drinks.

"Emilio Sagze," he said by way of thanks, and he offered a tender handshake. "Call me Gus."

Lucas called himself Roy Rogers. They drank in silence. When next he heard Sagze's voice, it was in a bantering tone with nasal anxiety.

"Fuck Mary Poppins."

"How?"

"Missionary. She won't do it no other way."

It was not auspicious. Lucas turned to Sagze and guessed aloud that he was from the Bronx and twenty-eight:

"Twenty-five," said Gus. "I'm younger than I look."

And his mother had given birth to him late, when she was in her forties. Lucas soon knew the rest.

"Why am I tellin' you all this?"

Lucas shrugged.

"I know," said Gus. "You said you was in film."

"That's it," said Lucas.

When he was fourteen, Gus had produced his first pornographic film. It starred his girl friend and the left end from his high school football team. He charged his friends fifty cents apiece to watch it in the basement. They enjoyed it, and Gus himself was excited to see his ostensibly prissy Liz Crayon take on Wally Rutgers.

"She had 'em out to here," said Gus.

Gus made more and better films. He couldn't handle the camera himself because of his eyesight and glasses, but if he entrusted the cinematography to somebody else, the movies were likely to be in focus. They were only a few minutes long and could be used in peepshows. He sold them as loops to his uncle for expenses plus sixty dollars. Occasionally he acted himself in these films, but there was a certain power to be retained by staying behind the scenes. What pleased him most of all was to be able to give part of the money to his mother. His father had moved to Mexico and never sent the support payments.

"A mother is a guy's best friend," Gus told Lucas. "And that ain't no joke."

When he was just twenty years old, Gus went partners with a photographer in a mail order business. He wrote the copy for the ads that appeared in the magazines:

B O R E D?

> I've got what you really
> want to see. Wide open,
> you bet! Don't be shy, it
> don't become you. Conf.
> reply + 4 sample photos.
> $2, no stamps please.
> JOANIE   Box 243 NY36

Gus made his girl friends write the letters, which he dictated, on scented stationery. He enclosed some photos, and if anybody wrote back and sent the $25 she asked for, he got two dozen snapshots and a personal letter begging for more.

"One guy in Ohio got a fetish on this girl who was my best friend," said Gus. "He sent her enough dough and she went out and saw him. He only had one leg. He had this scrapbook with all her pictures in it. She gave him a lock of her pussy and balled him once. She came back and went to work in a bank. I don't see her no more."

Gus Sagze had known that he was going to dedicate his life to the sex world ever since he was a little guy. By 1975 he wanted to do something really big. He decided to produce a great movie, like *Deep Throat* or *Memphis Cathouse*. He thought about it day and night.

"You ever read *Faust*?"

Lucas shook his head. "Actually, no."

"You should."

Gus was familiar with the Faust story because he had read part of it in high school and seen a version performed by puppeteers. He identified with it.

"I was gonna get Cheri Bomb to play Margaret," said Gus.

"That's a great idea."

Gus sipped his drink, raised high his glass. "Yet, without any jesting or joking, I tell you that this young beauty can't be had so easy. It depends less on passion than on coming."

"Good," said Lucas.

"I had a writer lined up, cameraman, everything. Girls, guys."

"So?"

"It went bust."

He didn't explain why, however. It seemed that Gus had been forced out of pornography altogether. Lucas suspected that the Mafia had moved in because Gus said that he had got too big, and then he stared disconsolately into his drink.

"What do you do these days?" asked Lucas.

"I'm a flower arranger. Daisy chains, mostly."

The bar closed early, and that night there was a stabbing in the telephone booth. Gus and Lucas left together near midnight before the police arrived.

"It was nice meeting ya, pal."

Gus had to take the train home. Now he lived in Flushing, in a little house across from the cemetery on Utopia Parkway. Lucas walked him to the subway.

And went with him.

Lucas was not so surprised. It was entirely by chance, for which he had great respect. The intuition was completely unconscious. He could have roamed the world over and found a hundred Sagzes, and a million imitations. In the middle of Utopia Parkway, at one-thirty in the morning, Gus turned to ask him:

"What's your perversion?"

Lucas shrugged.

"Everybody's got one."

The porch light was still burning when they mounted the steps, and the door was opened by a woman Gus introduced as Kitty.

"Kitty, meet Roy Rogers," he said. "How's Mama?"

"Asleep," said Kitty. She was a diminutive, oddly beautiful young woman. In the muted hallway light she stared at Lucas cautiously. She was wearing tight black jeans and a leather vest over a skimpy top. She had olive skin and short black hair parted in the middle.

"Get us some drinks," said Gus.

They entered a small living room which looked through a short hallway to the kitchen. In the kitchen stood a crib, and Gus caught Lucas staring at it.

"That's where Mama stays," said Gus. "Since she got senile."

Lucas sat down on a chair. The house smelled of disinfectant.

"She can't talk no more," said Gus sadly. "She

just makes sounds. Used to be so cheerful, too. She was a saint when I was a kid. Some people say I should put her away in, you know, a home. But how can a guy do that?''

"No," Lucas nodded slowly.

"She busts a gut to raise a fella and then he's gonna treat her like a fuckin' toothache? Not in my book."

Kitty came through the hallway carrying glasses and a bottle of coconut liqueur. She closed a door on the kitchen, leaving the living room cramped, ill-lighted, claustrophobic. She poured drinks and asked Gus:

"Where does he come from?"

"He's in film," said Gus. He crumbled onto the davenport.

Kitty pushed aside his feet and sat beside him, primly. She sipped the milky liquid and asked Lucas, "You want me to whip you?"

Lucas smiled. "No, thanks."

"Kitty is a dominatrice in her spare time," explained Gus.

"And spare time is all I've got." She had a Midwest accent.

"She's been stepping on men's backs since she was twelve," said Gus.

"My mother was a dominatrice, too," nodded Kitty. "You could say I followed in her footsteps."

"It was your stepmother," reminded Gus.

"Argue with me," said Kitty. She pointed to Lucas. "What kind of pervert is he?"

"He wouldn't tell me," said Gus.

"You brought him home."

"Then he ain't a faggot." Gus leaned forward,

his glasses almost falling off. "Come on, Roy Rogers," he grinned. "Rubber sports? Cross dressing? Greek, Roman? Cropo-cop—"

"Coprophilia," said Kitty demurely.

"What's that other one? Urolagnia?"

"Right," said Kitty. "Good. Piss on me."

"No," said Lucas. "None of those."

"Maybe he wants you to talk dirty," suggested Gus. "Kitty's real good at that."

"I am not," said Kitty. "But I'm improving."

Gus still stared and grinned. "Old ladies? Fat women? Little girls?"

Lucas nodded abruptly. Gus caught it and held his tongue. Lucas leaned forward, clasping his hands. He licked his dry lips. "Little girls, yes."

Gus sat up. *All right!*"

"Gus says everybody's got a perversion," said Kitty. "I guess he just found yours."

"I'm like a very important pervert," laughed Gus. His laughter had a delighted childish quality. He sat up straight and cracked his knuckles. He was excited. Just a flower arranger, but there were moments when he felt like a VIP. "Kitty here is twenty-two. I guess that's too old, huh?"

"By about ten years," said Kitty. "Right?"

"Right," said Lucas. He felt suddenly electric. He felt like a man with lightning in his fingertips. Nothing was certain. Cautiously, he waited.

"How young you want 'em?" asked Gus. "I know how you can buy the whole package real young. I—"

Lucas was shaking his head. Why was that? Gus wondered.

"You don't want to buy it, huh? They're expensive,

I know. I know how to set ya up with a little girl, but it costs every shot. Ya got a father complex or somethin'? Whatever you want—"

"Unload," said Lucas quietly.

"I can always get her for ya wholesale. What did you say?" Gus Sagze stared at him.

"I'm tired of her," said Lucas. Both Gus and Kitty leaned closer. "I want to get rid of her."

"How—how old?"

"Fourteen."

Kitty sprang up. "I can see it in his eyes, Gus."

"You are one sick motherfucker," said Gus.

"Really sick," added Kitty.

There was a short silence that would have alerted a leopard in a nylon jungle. Gus Sagze went rigid. To Kitty he said shortly:

"Get out."

Kitty was rigid, too. "Fuck you," she breathed.

"Get out now."

"She's not trained or anything," said Lucas.

Kitty took her drink and walked. As she passed Lucas, she leaned down toward his eyes. "There's just one thing I've got to say to you, mister."

"What's that?"

"You're really sick."

ELEVEN

The two men waited until after the last show on a
Saturday night. The introductions took place along
the runway at the Roxy. Phyllis emerged from the
dressing room, and one of them stepped forward and
asked for a word. Phyllis could give them a word.
She had noticed them earlier, from the stage while
she danced, and she had guessed, from Lucas's
description, that one might be Gus Sagze. The guy in

the brushed denim leisure suit looked like he had
been run over by a truck and wore thick glasses. His
mouth was unusually long.

The other man held back. He looked awkward,
was slight, and also wore glasses. In the theater, its
lights down and the place smelling of semen and
sweat and marijuana, it was Gus Sagze who offered
Phyllis a gracious hand with a leer:

"Emilio," he smiled. "How are ya?"

Phyllis nodded that she was okay and took out a
cigarette, which Gus lit for her with a slim lighter.
He pointed to the man behind him.

"Just a friend of mine."

Phyllis waved the cigarette in his direction. The
slight man sat in the shadows with his legs crossed
and his hands a steeple.

"You're good," said Emilio.

"Thanks."

"I mean, good."

Phyllis hoisted herself onto the runway between
the footlights and dangled her feet. It had been a long
night. Phyllis didn't have a headache because she had
taken six aspirin at midnight with a little Tab, but she
was tired. From dancing she was a little dazed, as a
matter of fact. But she knew that she was about to
have an important conversation. About slavery. Lucas had said she didn't even have to act, probably.
She watched Emilio light his own cigarette. Emilio
Sagze, but everybody called him Gus—Phyllis remembered.

"Caldonia, right?"

"Uh-huh."

Phyllis watched his hand tentatively circle her thigh,
squeeze it, then drop it to his side and make a fist.

The fist dropped the index finger and it came up to point at her.

"You got it."

"What?"

Emilio turned to the man behind him. "She asks what, right?"

"What?" asked Phyllis again.

"Sex appeal." Emilio showed an ingratiating smile.

"Oh." Phyllis blew a smoke ring. "That." Come on, she thought. Was this white slavery? This would be easy.

"What's wrong with sex appeal?" asked Sagze.

"I didn't say anything was."

"You bet. And you got it." He put his nose up and glanced around. "It smells crummy in here."

"It always smells like this."

"Yeah?"

"Uh-huh."

He walked away from her. He adjusted his glasses, then took them off to blow on them, and put them back on. He wiped his mouth, then wiped his slacks with his hands. He put his hands in his pockets and began to pace. From ten paces he called out: "How much do ya make in this place?"

Phyllis called back. "What you want to know for?"

"Just tell me. Two hundred?"

"More."

"Three?"

"Maybe."

Sagze came through the aisle, still with an outrageous grin on his broad mouth. "You can double it." As if it were such a serious thing to say to someone, he repeated himself.

"How?"

He turned to his friend sitting in the shadows again. "She asks, how."

The stranger unlocked the steeple his hands made. Coldly he said, "So, tell her."

Sagze dropped his hand to her thigh again. He left it there and Phyllis could soon feel its warmth. It was pale with dark hair; the fingers were thick. "You can come to work for me."

"I can?" Phyllis dropped her cigarette, and Sagze graciously found the butt on the floor and stepped on it. Phyllis thanked him. The Roxy was a firetrap.

"I got a club over on Lexington Avenue," said Sagze. "The Horizons. Nice place. Ever heard of it?"

"No."

"I got dancers like you. I pay 'em all six hundred a week. You're good, you got sex appeal. You'll make more than that even."

Phyllis smiled her thanks. It sounded good. She knew it was a ruse, and though she had got a lot of compliments since she'd been working in burlesque, it still sounded good. This was how she had started turning tricks in Bettendorf, Rock Island, East Moline, and—

"What do I have to do?" she asked.

"What I seen you do in this place," said Sagze. "That's all."

It was all too familiar. "Just dance?"

Sagze stiffened slightly. "Yeah. Just dance." He adjusted his glasses. Behind him, the stranger in the shadows cleared his throat. Sagze turned and stared.

"What's the matter with you?"

The stranger didn't reply.

"For just dancing?" asked Phyllis again.

"Well," said Sagze slowly. "You do hand jobs, too."

Phyllis stared at him. Hand jobs, too.

"Guys come in," said Sagze, with a touch of business pride, "all nice guys in suits, nothin' crappy. They have a drink or two at the bar and see you dance. Then the both of you go in the back. We got nice little rooms there, you can give 'em hand jobs."

"Six hundred a week?"

"Yeah." Sagze shrugged. "I give you fifty a day. You work the rest on tips. All my girls make at least six-fifty."

"I'll bet they—"

"Sometimes the guys want a little mouth work, too, you know?" He touched the knot of his tie. "But that's up to you."

Phyllis looked away. She was confused. This couldn't be the right ruse for white slavery. Lucas had said to expect the world on a silver plate; that's what she thought, too. But here was Sagze, calling himself Emilio—and how many Emilios do you meet in one day?—offering her a job as a cheap whore. Maybe Lucas didn't have it right. She wondered.

"You can screw the guys," continued Sagze, "but don't tell me about it. We got little kind of cots in them rooms." He didn't seem to want to look at her, either. "But no robberies. You can't fleece 'em. That ain't straight and they won't come back."

"No?"

"No dirty pool," said Sagze.

Right now hand jobs didn't appeal to Phyllis. She didn't want any mouth work either. She didn't care to screw the guys. Sagze in the dim light had taken on a hovering, threatening presence, had acquired it suddenly with his broad, weasly mouth. It was three in the morning. She wanted to go home. Maybe Lucas could straighten out this mess. It was the wrong ruse. Phyllis put her cigarettes in her shoulder bag and put the bag over her shoulder. She dropped from the runway onto the floor.

"I can think about it, right?"

Sagze's face expressed disappointment. "I'm makin' you this offer—"

"And I'm gonna think about it," said Phyllis, annoyed. "But now I got to go."

She set her lips and slipped by him. She thought she was free but he grabbed her wrist.

"Hey—Caldonia—what's wrong?"

"Let me go!"

Sagze pulled her back to him like a yo-yo. He leered. "You'd do a nice hand job, wouldn't ya?"

"Not for you," said Phyllis. "Or mouth work, either."

"Maybe you could start now." Sagze squeezed her wrist and snaked an arm around her neck beneath her hair. "Maybe—"

She bit him. She snapped her head away and bit his hand. She tasted blood. It had no taste at all. He gasped in pain.

She jerked free and started to run. She couldn't make it to the door if he chased her. He did chase her. She could make it to the runway and backstage. She ran for the utility steps. When Sagze caught her, he was salivating in earnest.

"You little witch." He thrust her up against a

pillar. It was the same pillar that gave so many patrons of the Roxy a neck cramp trying to look around it. Gus Sagze put a knee in her stomach and ripped her bag off her shoulder and tossed it. He grappled with her and got both wrists within his one bleeding hand. With his other hand he pulled at her hair by the roots and put his face close to hers.

"You deserved it," said Phyllis. She was getting ready to spit at him.

"You bit me." Still astonished, Sagze said it again. "For Christ almighty."

"Get off me," hissed Phyllis.

"You bitch," he hissed back. "Don't you know that human bites—"

Phyllis heard a shuffling behind him. Then quiet words: "Emilio. Enough."

"She's got me bleeding," said Sagze. "I could get lockjaw for Christ's sake."

"You couldn't do any mouth work then," jeered Phyllis.

"Let her go, Emilio."

"Your mother's ass," said Sagze.

Behind Emilio Phyllis could see nothing. She looked up, though, and saw a hand reach over the top of Sagze's head. It pulled up his slick black hair and ripped his head backwards.

First he screamed in pain. Then he let go of Phyllis. The stranger stepped to one side, brought a foot between Sagze's two, and tripped him. He sent Sagze sprawling into the aisle.

After a short silence in the dark Roxy Theater— where there was neither a bartender nor a cowpoke in sight—Gus Sagze got up silently. He dusted himself off. His brushed denim had blood on it, from his hand, and it was dirty. His glasses were gone, and when he couldn't see to find them, he kicked the backs of chairs in despair.

The stranger, seeing the glasses on the floor, kicked them Sagze's way. Sagze groped for them on the floor and, when he found them, put them on and adjusted them. Without looking at anybody, he left the theater.

Phyllis broke into sobs. It wasn't acting. Lucas said she wouldn't have to. Her stomach hurt, her wrists were in pain, her mouth still tasted Sagze's blood. She had a right to cry.

"What's your name, Caldonia?" The slender man in glasses, the stranger, was in the aisle, putting Phyllis's bag back together.

"Phyllis." She picked up Emilio's bloody handkerchief and found a white corner. "Phyllis."

"Where are you from, Phyllis?"

"Rock Island." She dabbed her eyes. "And Moline, East Moline and Bettendorf and Davenport."

"Been in New York long?"

"Not long."

He brought her the bag, presented it to her dangling from his fingers. "Maybe if there's anything missing, you can come find it tomorrow." He smiled.

"Thanks."

"You live nearby?"

"Forty-third."

"Emilio gets pretty small at times."

"I didn't mean to bite him," said Phyllis. "But he held onto me."

"Don't worry about it. If I know Emilio, he'll find

somebody to lick his wounds.'' He offered Phyllis a small hand to shake. His grip was weak but pleasant; his palm was cool and dry. "Jonathan," he said. He pointed to a corner of his mouth, as a gesture she had blood on her own. She wiped it off.

"You're his friend?"

"I was," said Jonathan. "I don't know about now."

"Do you own the Horizon, too?"

Jonathan shook his head. "No, I'm just in town for a visit. Emilio's an old wayward friend. I'm from around Palm Beach."

"Florida?"

"Gatorland," he nodded.

"Alligators and crocodiles."

"Ever been there?"

"No."

"Your boyfriend should take you sometime." Jonathan gestured to the rafters. "It is kind of smelly in here, though. Emilio was right about that."

"Yeah." Phyllis grimaced. "It is."

They began to walk together toward the illuminated EXIT sign. Jonathan was not much taller than Phyllis, and she glanced at him sidelong. His face in the yellow light was pleasant and had relaxed into middle age, and his gentle smile seemed always there. His hands in his pockets, he wore a yellow fedora pushed way back on his head.

"I'll walk you home," he suggested, "unless you're meeting someone."

"No—"

"Your boyfriend might be the jealous type—"

Phyllis stopped on the stairs with her hand on the

old brass rail. "What makes you think I got an old man?"

Jonathan shrugged. "I thought Emilio said something. That was why we were—"

"Emilio knows Roy?"

"That was it." Jonathan pointed a finger at her. "And we should come—"

"That son of a bitch." Phyllis pounded a small curled fist on the old plaster wall. "No, it's not your fault," she said, pouting. "It's just that my old man just kicked me out."

"Oh, I'm sorry—"

"Don't be," said Phyllis. They began to walk down the stairs. She gritted her teeth. "Kicks me out and then sends over that fucking creep. Like I'm just another whore."

Jonathan held open the door for her. "I'm sure it was something else—"

"You don't know my old boyfriend," said Phyllis.

Jonathan checked his watch. They were outside now, in the middle of a gentle, warm night. They walked toward Broadway. "Listen, maybe I'd better get you a cab."

Phyllis stopped short. "I thought you were gonna walk me home."

"Well, I just noticed—" Jonathan Barnes smiled apologetically. "It's late and I really have to get something to eat. I don't suppose you'd know a nice place that's open all night?"

"Childs only—"

"Maybe you'd like a bite, too," he said. "Where are my manners, anyway? Come on, be my—"

"No," said Phyllis. "I'll buy."

"Don't be silly."

"No. You just maybe saved my life."

Jonathan raised his hand to fetch a Checker cab that was barreling down Broadway. "I wouldn't say that."

TWELVE

He would have liked to have wrung her little neck
and sent her to Palm Beach in a plastic bag. Air
Express. But patience won out, as it almost always
did. A late night snack wasn't enough to get the girl
Phyllis. He had to see her again, and buy her dinner.
And it couldn't be the next night, either. He had to
be busy. Monday night, then. But wouldn't she be
tired? Maybe they'd just have to forget it. No—it
was early in the week, wasn't it?

"Monday, then," he agreed reluctantly.

"Oh, I'll like that," she said.

Jonathan Barnes smiled. Inwardly his stomach churned. Little Phyllis Lantern was going to keep him in New York another few days. He gazed into her pretty, transparent eyes, which he wanted to gouge out with an icepick. At least she was a cute little blonde. They were at a premium these days. Barrezia would be highly satisfied and stamp her FRAGILE all over. Money was money. Flesh was also money.

"Where will we meet?"

Maybe he could just sleep and watch cable television until they had dinner and he got her. Or he could check in on Quinta Mechanic and see how she was doing with Lucas Jameson—it had been a while now. A restaurant:

"The China Bowl," he said. "Seven-thirty."

"I'll be there," said Phyllis.

The method Jonathan Barnes used to procure women was always about the same. And yet each time was a little different—almost, he thought, as if one girl differed from the next. Phyllis Lantern was old enough to be taken to dinner; she sounded as if she had a few street smarts. Her I.Q. was probably above 80 and maybe she knew what an isosceles triangle was. He met her at the China Bowl and bribed the waiter to bring her a Singapore sling.

"They're not too sweet," he said. "But just one is enough."

He had already heard about her background, so they made small talk through the chow mein. He had been married once, he admitted, but his wife had left him. There were no children, thank heavens. It took him a long time to get over it, and that was when he had moved back with his mother. In the springtime— just now, in fact—he liked to take long canoeing trips in the Everglades. If it weren't for this convention of math teachers—and were they ever boring—he would be there now. Florida was a nice place for trips like that—

"But I can see you like New York."

Phyllis shrugged.

"You keep thinking of getting away."

"That's it," she smiled.

"Have you ever thought about . . . going back?"

He meant Rock Island, even if it was where her father had died.

"Sometimes. It's just . . ." Phyllis stared disconsolately into her tea.

"I shouldn't." Jonathan shook his head. "You see, I never had a baby sister."

He noticed she glanced up quickly, almost suspiciously, but he kept talking. His mother had wanted a little girl to round out the family after he was born. That was when his father had died.

"Not everything happens the way we want," he said pointedly, longingly.

"You can say that again." Phyllis grimaced.

"At least you have a talent," said Jonathan.

"A tal—"

Her dancing. He did think she was a good dancer, with potential. How would he know, anyway? she might ask. But his mother had been a dancer. In fact, she had been friends with the famous ecdysiast, Honey Bee.

"Ecdysiast—"

"A stripteaser," grinned Phyllis.

She *was* smart. He would be careful. He smiled: "It's from the Greek *ekdysis*. It means to get out, to molt."

Yes, the famous ecdysiast. Just a high school math teacher himself, Jonathan often thought about *getting out*. Who wouldn't? But there was his mother to think of; she still taught dance classes, but didn't make much money.

"Your mother *teaches* dancing?" asked Phyllis.

"We're all teachers in my family," said Jonathan, with a touch of pride. "She teaches . . . ecdysis!" He laughed.

"Does she have many students?"

"Too many." Jonathan shook his head. "Everybody wants to learn to dance the way you and my mother do it. But hardly anybody knows how to teach it."

"I can see that," said Phyllis. "Yeah."

"It's like everything else." He shrugged. "It's too bad you're only thirt—"

"Fourteen," said Phyllis.

"Well, if you were older," he said, "you could teach better than a lot of them, probably."

"Oh, I don't—"

"I know. Believe me, you could." He sipped his tea. "She had a fifteen-year-old who wanted to teach, just last year, as a matter of fact."

"What happened?"

He lighted the girl's cigarette. "She was too young."

When the waiter came with the fortune cookies, Phyllis cracked hers and showed it to Jonathan. The tag read BEST NEWS COME NOW YET.

"Well, I want to get out of New York," said Phyllis. "That's for sure."

"Of course . . ." Jonathan drew out his words slowly, "Mother does sometimes hire sixteen-year-olds. But only as assistants."

"Assistants?" Phyllis crossed her legs and sat up self-consciously.

"They aren't paid as much as teachers," said Jonathan. "But sometimes they work professionally on the side. It's sort of a steppingstone."

"I'll say—it sounds—"

"I doubt she needs one now, though."

"That's too bad," said Phyllis. "I bet I could—"

Jonathan glanced up sharply. "I'm not trying to—"

"Oh, I know you weren't," said Phyllis. "I was just thinking how I've had experience and—"

"That's true," admitted Jonathan. He busied himself with the bill. He paid in cash, the exact amount with change from a small purse, and added a ten percent tip. "Where were we?"

"I *have* had experience."

Jonathan said dubiously, "I could call her and see, I suppose."

That was the ticket. She had to gush with excitement. She did.

"Would you? I mean, it would be wonderful!"

He stalled. He pointed out that it was ten o'clock at night. His mother was probably getting ready for bed. She did like to watch the news, however. Perhaps Phyllis could think about it while he went to the men's room. He lingered in the men's room, examining his new grey hairs beneath the fluorescent light. At the table the waiter had taken away his tea. He wanted another cup. Where was his napkin? He wanted sugar with his tea. Chinese restaurants could be difficult. He turned to her.

"I guess, if you wanted, I could give her a call."

"I'd really appreciate it," said Phyllis. She was flush with excitement.

"All right," he finally assented. "I'll be right back."

But before he was halfway across the room, he turned back. He saw her face fall. He shook his head.

"Look, I've got a better idea," he said.

"If it's any—"

"Why don't *you* talk to her?"

Phyllis jumped at the chance. Jonathan could see her hanging from the Chinese lanterns, her little body twisting slowly as the waiters put away the knives and forks. He smiled broadly. Together they went to the telephones.

"Let me—"

"No, I have it." Jonathan counted out the correct change from his purse, then started to dial. He moved his hand and the purse dropped to the floor, spilling the rest of his silver.

"Would you pick that up?"

By the time Phyllis stood up, he had dialed the number and it was ringing. When Sylvia answered, he was smiling at her.

"Mother . . . No, I'm fine. . . ."

For a few minutes he spoke to her. She had been to the dog track that day. He had bought her some skin lotion at Kiehl's. The convention was boring. Finally, *There's a young woman here, Mother—she's only sixteen but I thought—*

Suddenly he handed Phyllis the telephone. Only then did it occur to the girl that she didn't know his last name. She said, "Mrs.—"

"Just ask if it's Twilight Star," said Jonathan. "That was her stage name." He stood close while she talked. He could hear his mother's lovely Southern accent.

"Oh, call me Sylvia, honey. Twilight Star—that's so long ago. That boy of mine ... ."

They chatted for a moment. Jonathan detested women nattering together. He closed his eyes.

"How long have you been dancing, honey?"

Sylvia could become quite businesslike when she wanted. Phyllis had to tell her how long, and where, and who she had worked with. And, "Don't tell me your age, honey, but do you have any employment papers?"

Phyllis blanched. She glanced sharply at Jonathan and mouthed the words: *Employment papers*.

"Say yes," whispered Jonathan. "I'll take care of it."

"Yes, I do, Mrs.—"

"Because—I'm so glad you called—it just so happens, I *may* have a spot in a few days. One of the girls—she's my best girl, a doll—got a job at Vegas. And you know, she just sprang the news on me yesterday. Isn't that the way everything is? It leaves me in kind of a—well, I don't want to say a bind."

"Oh, I'm sorry," said Phyllis. "I—"

"I tell you what. If you could come *right away*—"

"Right—"

"In the very next day or two—you know what I mean. You don't have to hop the first plane a-flying, you understand. But in the next—"

"Oh, I could do that," said Phyllis. "I'm sure I could."

"Why, then, I believe we could find a place out here."

"That w—"

"You have relatives out this way?"

"No, I—"

"Well, that's a problem. I could put you up for a few days, I guess. Not for *too* long, but—"

"I could stay in a ho—"

"Don't you *think* about staying in a motel now." Sylvia clucked audibly. "First you come on out and get your bearings. I don't know what that Yankee living does to folks. But say, you don't have a dog or cat or nothing like that?"

"No—I don't have—any pets," said Phyllis. Jonathan looked down. Her fingers were crossed.

"Because I *am* allergic."

"I don't have any—"

"And Phyllis? Now, I know you have the money, what you working and all. But you let my Jonathan buy your ticket, hear? See, I can take it off my taxes as a business deduction."

"Oh, thanks b—"

"That'll be the Palm Beach Airport. I'll pick you up. You just get it straight and Jonathan'll tell me when your flight is. And remember about the ticket. Better let me talk to that boy . . ."

Breathless, Phyllis handed the phone back. Jonathan was smiling broadly as he accepted the receiver, and said, "Now tell me I'm not a good son!"

THIRTEEN

Lucas took snapshots of Jonathan Barnes in the China Bowl. They were dark, exposed without a flash, and badly focused. Phyllis stole Jonathan's teacup. His fingerprints went nowhere: he had no criminal record; he had never been in the Army.

She was to leave on Wednesday morning. Jonathan, once he had her, wasted no time. He would meet her at the airport and give her the ticket he had gone out of his way to purchase. She was free to back out. His congenial nonchalance insured that she would not.

On Tuesday afternoon Lucas took her on a carriage ride through Central Park. It was early May. Pine warblers and laughing gulls nested in the sweet birch and sugar maple still flowering. The carriage was closed and the drapes were drawn. It was drizzling. He put his arms around her and whispered in her ear.

"You may get killed."

He was testing her resolve. He had to keep his ulcers from perforating. They were in his mind, not his stomach. She took one of his hands between her own.

"They won't touch me. Or maybe only a little. You said yourself I must be worth twenty thousand at least."

Phyllis had impressed herself as an actress. Even Lucas had said she would go a long way. Jonathan clearly had believed everything she told him. Of course, he wasn't so bad himself. Phyllis added:

"Besides, Jonathan's not like you think."

"We've been through that," said Lucas, annoyed. "It was a ruse, all of it."

"I know. But Emilio or Sagze—or whoever he is—he's an animal."

"Jonathan's worse."

Phyllis held out for Jonathan's marginal involvement in this white slavery. It was strange, but there was a part of her which believed in him. She saw right through him, and yet there was this recurrent fantasy, which she couldn't shake, that at worst Jonathan had a scheme to con her out of some money, or to get her to dance for free. Since the night before, when she'd returned to the hotel flush with excitement, she had been exclaiming to Lucas:

"I mean, he let me talk to his *mother*."

"I bet she was real nice."

"Tops—" A note of confusion came into her voice. "What if this is all . . . for nothing?"

Lucas was displeased. He didn't know why. He felt himself to be somehow sinister and ugly. Peering through the curtains in the carriage, he saw that they were passing the old carousel, at 65th Street. They still had time. "Again," he said to Phyllis. He smiled dimly and squeezed her hand. "Let's go over it once more."

Phyllis sighed. Lucas could be a trial. She said, "I get up at six tomorrow morning and go to the airport. LaGuardia."

"Right."

"You follow me separately—are you going to pack anything?"

"It's hot in Florida," nodded Lucas. "Go on."

"I leave on the eight o'clock flight to Palm Beach, which arrives at eleven-fifteen. I meet Sylvia." She glanced ruefully at Lucas. "Jonathan's *mother*."

"Fat chance."

"Everybody has one, Lucas, you should know."

"I do know."

"And then I guess we go to her house and—I don't know after that."

"Nobody does," said Lucas.

"It's a simple plan," said Phyllis hollowly. "You're on the same flight I am. I have a checked bag and you don't. In Palm Beach there's a car waiting for you. You follow—"

"And what else?"

"Oh. A detective waiting, too. Because—in case Jonathan waits around and you can't—"

"In case I have to take the next flight."

"And also because a good tail—" She laughed briefly. "A good tail utilizes two cars."

Lucas sighed. It was a good plan; it was somehow lousy. He had contacted a detective agency in Palm Beach. Sam Spade would be waiting. Something was wrong."

"And where will it end?" asked Phyllis rhetorically.

"I don't know."

It was beginning to dawn on Lucas that he did not know, had never known, when or where it would end. White slavery was like the old tapeworm cure. You lured the tapeworm up the esophagus and out the mouth with a dish of milk. But you couldn't bite down until the whole organism was out in the open, or else it went báck down into the stomach and kept multiplying. The Piper was down there. The men who trained young girls—and boys, too, probably. And the pedophiles who bought them.

He was in the dark, anyway, he supposed, but there was Phyllis to help him illumine these little crimes. And also his feeling for her, to muddy his vision. Despite her ambivalence toward Jonathan, she had performed almost flawlessly. The better she stood up, the more he liked her. There were moments when he stepped back, in fact, to tell himself he didn't love her. He no longer thought of her as fourteen or any age at all. It was astonishing. He probably was at one remove from the perverts he was trying to expose. He wondered if they reproached themselves the way he sometimes did himself. Since the night he had met Gus Sagze, the words of the poet Ducasse kept coming into his head: *I am vile. Lice gnaw me. When vermin look at me they vomit.* He shuddered when he considered that, in sum, the requirement was only that he treat his feelings for the girl with the same cold-blooded detachment as others would. As slavers would. He was vile. He could feel the lice—

"Lucas?"

"Just thinking."

She nestled closer to him. He put his arms around her and kissed her. Her lips were soft, pliant, and working.

Late that same afternoon Jonathan Barnes got tired of watching cable television. He left his room in the Hotel Tudor and walked across 42nd Street to Grand Central Station. From a telephone booth he reached Luis Barrezia at home.

"Goosie-goosie-goo," he said.

"Ha! Jonathan." Barrezia chuckled. "Am eating breakfast."

Jonathan sighed. Barrezia had to watch his weight. He didn't need breakfast at any time of day. "You can tell Sylvia I'm sending her a package."

"Yes? Tell me. American product?"

"That's right," said Jonathan. "And in working order."

Barrezia always liked this little game. "There is nothing better than American craftsmanship. Is difficult to make work sometimes, but it brings us very high price."

"This one especially," grinned Jonathan. "The cock goes in before the name comes off."

"Precisely. How many years?"

"Fourteen."

"Not bad."

"Blonde."

"Good."

"Tell Sylvia I'll call her myself once the freight is on board."

"I will do this," said Barrezia. After a pause he asked, "What about Lucky Jimsom?"

"Lucas Jameson," corrected Jonathan. "Still working on it."

"Quinta Mechanic?"

"Yes."

Barrezia sighed with apparent satisfaction. That ended their conversation. Jonathan hung up the telephone. He felt restless and didn't want to go back to his hotel room. He didn't know what to do. It was rush hour. In the end he wandered down to the Oyster Bar and had some clams.

And that night, at the Venus Lounge, Lucas Jameson sat abandoned in a dark corner, nursing a colorful Pernod. There was no quitting. There was no jumping down. Phyllis Lantern stood at the bar, at one dark end of it, drinking a ginger ale. She was talking to Louise Cole, who stood beside her, staring into a phosphorescent brandy.

". . . and I talked to his mother, too," Phyllis was saying. She tried to reason her confusion out with the old woman. Jonathan was a math teacher. Of course, she had heard the baby sister routine before. And yet—

"He don't act like a pimp, you say?" asked Louise.

"Not a bit. And Lucas had Roscoe Gatling check out his fingerprints, and there aren't any. He doesn't have a conviction record."

"No?"

"That's why I'm thinking maybe it's just a scam to get me—"

"There's a million dough-rollin' scams, aren't there?"

"That's what I told Lucas."

Louise grimaced and took a drink. Her lips pursed as it settled down her throat. She turned her head. "What am I looking at?"

Phyllis shivered. "Me."

"You. A chicken. All dressed up and ready to cook. You know what—"

"Louise—"

"Know what a wooden kimono is?"

Phyllis shook her head.

"A coffin box. Listen here." The old woman reached up with both her hands. Phyllis flinched, as though she would be struck. But Louise took her face between her hands and shook her head. "Them with mothers is the worst. They'll bite off your head without thinking. You won't be nothin' when they're through."

Phyllis felt the warm hands on her face. "I won't—"

"All you'll be is a dead chicken," said Louise. "A dead chicken in a wooden kimono, that's all."

FOURTEEN

Quinta Mechanic was waiting for Lucas Jameson to return to his apartment in the Colonnades. She had been virtually living there for about three weeks, and so far he had remained away. This didn't concern her unduly because there were a half dozen unpaid and overdue bills in his mailbox, including an angry letter from Con Edison. His telephone rang at all odd hours of the night, which sometimes annoyed her. But

Quinta reasoned that Lucas Jameson was due back soon. She had not been hired to go searching for him. She had been retained for something else, and when he got back, she would do it.

It had been Quinta's experience that if you stayed in a person's dwelling about seventy percent of the time, there was little likelihood of missing him or her; otherwise, your time was your own. With Lucas Jameson, especially, this presented no problem. Quinta had waited for men in some of the most disgusting hovels on earth, she felt, and not just a few weeks but a month or more at a time. The mud hut in Algeria had been the filthiest, but the apartment in the South Bronx had been the most physically repellent. Once Quinta had waited for the president of a liquor company in his Fifth Avenue apartment, where there was a great deal to drink, if you were a drinker, but nothing whatsoever to read. Quinta had felt a good deal like the mariner in Coleridge's poem, until she had ordered out to Brentano's.

Not only did Lucas Jameson leave plenty to read in his pleasant, but bare, apartment; there was also the Public Theater across the street. That spring there was a Bunuel retrospective. Each evening, Quinta would leave Lucas Jameson's apartment, cross the street, and buy two tickets to that night's performance. Her husband would meet her at seven-thirty. They would attend the early show, and afterwards dine at Lady Astor's. Of course, Quinta and Merrill had seen many of his films before, but it was a pleasure to see them again: *The Exterminating Angel, Viridiana, The Phantom of Liberty*. And no matter how many times she saw the infamous *L'Age d'or,* Quinta Mechanic still roared with laughter at the end of that film, when after a hundred and twenty days of Sodom, Jesus Christ himself emerges from the scandalous chateau. When she laughed like that, Merrill Robbins said he feared for her heart.

At dinner Quinta and Merrill discussed not only the films of Bunuel, but also the famous old Colonnades, and she amazed him with her thorough knowledge of that venerable structure, down to the last nook and cranny. It sounded as though she could have built the thing, the way she knew even the ventilating systems and air ducts.

"You'd be an awfully old lady then," Merrill told her.

"Yes," she said. "A hundred and fifty-three."

After dinner, on those days when she was waiting for Lucas, Quinta would sometimes go home with Merrill, other times not, depending upon whether hours away from his apartment would spoil her seventy percent. When she did not go home with him, he acquiesced cheerfully as she put him in a cab, and he didn't ask questions. Merrill Robbins never asked his wife about what she did or where she went. He considered her an artist and knew that her work was important—whatever it was. He also knew that she wouldn't tell him, whatever she did, and, finally, he suspected that it was much better not to know. It probably helped that he was not jealous, but he knew he had no reason to be.

On Tuesday evening, May 8, Quinta Mechanic and her husband had an especially pleasant evening. They saw *The Discreet Charm of the Bourgeoisie* and were both amazed that a director as old and prodigious as Luis Bunuel could continue to be fresh and original. Afterwards they both ordered coquilles St.

Jacques and shared a fine bottle of *Frascati*, the tingling white wine that Lady Astor's so thoughtfully stocked. They both decided against the mousse, but lingered over coffee an hour.

"How about coming home with me?" asked Merrill, on the steps of the restaurant. It was after midnight. He circled his wife's waist, and reached up and kissed her.

"I probably shouldn't." Quinta glanced down the street to the entrance to Lucas Jameson's apartment. "I should stay."

Merrill Robbins detected his wife's ambivalence. They hadn't gone home together for several nights running.

"Come on," he urged her playfully. "I'll show you something."

Quinta Mechanic was sure that her husband was never going to run out of something to show her. But she was worried about her seventy percent.

"Maybe," she said doubtfully. "I don't know."

"I tell you what," said Merrill. "We'll walk over to Gem Spa and pick up the morning paper and some Life Savers. You can think about it."

She took his hand and they began to stroll. It was a pleasant evening and there were even a few stars shining in old Manhattan. Quinta said:

"That's a good idea. Let me think about it, then."

FIFTEEN

Lucas waked promptly at six, when it was still dark, and showered and dressed. He would have let Phyllis sleep another hour—good-byes were unnecessary, inappropriate—but she was awake when he emerged from the bathroom. She stood naked before the mirror, rubbing sleep from her eyes.

"You're going back to your apartment?"

He nodded. "A few things, I need to get them."

"Be careful," she thought to say.

"And I'll see you at the airport."

Phyllis circled his waist. At the door she buried her head in his chest. "I'll *see* you there, but I won't *meet* you."

"Right."

"So, *adios*."

Her body was still very warm from sleep and he held her a moment more.

"Go," she said.

With Lucas gone, Phyllis washed, dressed, and packed quickly and efficiently. She wore dark blue stockings with a short purple skirt and leotard visible under a white blouse buttoned halfway up. Her eyes seemed lifeless, so she applied mascara. She took four aspirin with the dregs of a Tab from the night before. She made the six-thirty bus to LaGuardia.

Jonathan was waiting for her at the check-in counter, as they had arranged. Phyllis had never been to the airport and was a little late finding the right place. Jonathan smiled through his annoyance. He was dressed in a light blue suit with a crisp shirt and thin tie. He was clean-shaven and looking well-rested, if a little pale.

"I'm sorry to be late," she apologized.

"It's all right. The plane's a little late taking off." Jonathan kept smiling. "That's a big bag. We'll have to check it."

They stood in a line a few minutes. Jonathan already had the ticket in his hand and got a stub for the suitcase. "Mother called me last night."

"I hope she didn't change her mind."

"No, she's glad you're coming. If this works out, you'll be a big help to her. If it doesn't . . ." He shrugged good-naturedly. "Well, *que sera, sera*. Don't think you're obligated. I've known the woman all my life, and she can be trying sometimes."

"You think we'll get along?" asked Phyllis, with a tone of alarm.

He touched her elbow, and they turned in the direction of the gates. "Oh, sure. But she's an exacting teacher. Everybody says she requires a lot from her students and from the people who work for her."

"I'm sure she can teach me a lot."

"She says self-discipline is the key," said Jonathan.

They went single-file through the security monitor, and when the machine buzzed unpleasantly on Jonathan, he emptied his pockets. It was nothing but a small steel pen knife, and he joked about it with the attendant.

"How will I know her when I get there?" asked Phyllis.

"She knows you're a blonde, for one thing. But here." And Jonathan took out his wallet and opened the card case to a snapshot. "She's a real redhead. This picture is about five years old, but she still looks the same."

"She's pretty."

"She's my mother," smiled Jonathan.

They walked slowly into the gate area. Jonathan stopped to buy a newspaper and shook his head at the sensational headlines before folding it under his arm. Passing a parade of Hare Krishnas in their orange suits, smelling of incense, their heads shaven and in sandals, Jonathan laughed. Phyllis did, too.

"To each his own," said Jonathan. "I've got to say I never used to be able to stand them, but in the last few years I don't mind so much. I guess I'm getting more tolerant in my old age.''

"I think they're creeps," said Phyllis.

"Maybe, but they don't cause anybody much trouble. The worst thing they'll ever say is that you're a dog. One of them called me that once—a dog."

"Did you turn the other cheek?"

Jonathan put back his head and laughed. "No. I busted him in the chops."

"Like with Emilio?"

"Everybody's got their little curse," smiled Jonathan. "Mine must be my bad temper. Sometimes I just can't control it."

"I know what you mean," nodded Phyllis, looking around. "You can't help the way you feel."

They were walking casually, and as they reached the gate, the passengers were in a line and already boarding. Phyllis strained to find Lucas among them.

"I've already got your seat," Jonathan was saying. "You're by the window in the smoking section, is that all right?"

Phyllis missed a beat, before nodding. "That's fine."

"This is it." Jonathan still had the ticket in his hand. The passengers were almost all inside the plane now. "You better hurry. It's been a pleasure, Phyllis . . ."

She grasped his extended hand, which was cool and dry. Hers was moist. "Thanks for everything," she said.

"I'll see you soon enough," Jonathan reminded her. "I'm coming home myself, at the end of the week."

"Oh, that'll be great."

"You'd better hurry now."

He handed her the newspaper, then opened her hand and snapped a red, white, black, and blue ticket into it.

"Run fast," he said.

All Phyllis could see when she boarded the plane were the teeth of the stewardess, coming increasingly closer as she strode through the vestibule. Then the hands of the stewardess were splitting her boarding pass, and those teeth were gleaming again, in a perfect toothpaste smile, as she said:

"Welcome aboard! Thanks for flying American!"

Lucas had gone back to his apartment in the Colonnades.

He was being careful about it. He had the taxi drop him on Eighth Street. He bought a cup of coffee, punched a hole in the plastic lid, and drank it as he walked over to Lafayette. It was to be a cool day without rain. The sun was rising behind a cloud cover. The street was empty.

He entered the vestibule cautiously, not bothering to check the mailbox because there wouldn't be anything in it except bills and junk. He unlocked the door to his apartment. It seemed undisturbed. He was relieved.

In the bedroom he brought down a small, worn suitcase from the closet, and began to pack some light clothes—cotton pants, a couple of short-sleeved shirts, some sandals. It got hot in Florida. He packed automatically.

The first time Lucas could remember packing his clothes, he had been eight years old. He was on his way to military school. He was being sent there because he had tossed a lighted firecracker into a bin of goosefeathers that went on to burn down his father's ticking factory. It was insured, but that didn't prevent Bill Jameson from tossing Lucas across the parking lot. He landed on his chin beside a '55 Studebaker and bled upon the hood. His mother, on leave from the hospital, came to watch the fire. She held his hand and, while firemen scrambled to toss smoldering mattresses out the window, squeezed it gently as she told him:

"It was Adolphe Menjou. I didn't think he'd stoop so low. Radio waves!"

Lucas had grown practiced at packing and now, in the quiet apartment, accomplished it with the unthinking efficiency of a salesman on a circuit. With the lights off and the window shades down, it was dark. The cat did not come to greet him. He was not surprised.

The final thing to take was the camera. The cheap Times Square bargain with which he had taken pictures of Jonathan at the China Bowl had proved inadequate. But his old Minolta, which he had owned for a dozen years, was superb. He removed it from the case to load it. He slipped in a new battery, then unwrapped a new roll of film.

It was funny the way handling a camera made Lucas feel as though he was being watched. The curse of a paranoid mother. When he had loaded the camera, he locked it shut and reached for the lens cleaner. He couldn't shake the silly fantasy that someone was—

She stood in the doorway.

All he could say was, "You found the cat." And God, she was big. "Thanks."

Quinta Mechanic held Hudson in her arms, and he was warm and purring against her ample bosom. "He's a nice cat."

"His name is Hudson." Lucas nodded slowly. "He likes you."

"We've been getting along fine."

Lucas Jameson laid his old camera carefully on the bed. The woman in the doorway had a pleasant face, and she was attractively dressed in parachute pants and a flannel shirt. And God, was she big. Man or woman, Lucas couldn't remember when he had seen anyone so . . . voluminous.

"You shouldn't feed male cats that dry food," said Quinta. She let Hudson down to the floor and he stayed by her feet a moment, washing himself. "It's tough on their kidneys."

"He mostly eats mice," said Lucas.

Quinta Mechanic gestured to the suitcase on the bed. "Going on a trip?"

"Yes."

"A long one?"

"Just a short one."

"Narragansett's pretty this time of year."

"That's just where I was thinking of going."

"Really?" Quinta smiled. "Ever eat at the Coast Guard Inn?"

"Many times," nodded Lucas. "Often."

They were quiet for a moment, and Lucas stole a glance at the bedside clock. It was 6:45. He would have to be going soon.

Quinta Mechanic rolled up her shirtsleeves. Her conscience had been bothering her all night. She had gone home with Merrill, as it turned out. She'd had a pleasant time—and an exquisite moment, in fact—

but she didn't sleep well. Seventy percent, she kept thinking. She had waked before six and jogged downtown.

"Let's go in the living room," she said quietly.

Lucas had no objection to that. It wouldn't have meant much if he did. They went into the living room where the big windows had draperies that Quinta Mechanic closed carefully. She said:

"You've got some nice books."

"Thanks."

"I notice you have Jacques Rigaut's *Agence génèrale du suicide.*"

Her accent was quite good. "Why, yes."

"He was a friend of André Breton, who was a friend of Duchamp," said Quinta.

"That's true," admitted Lucas.

"And surrealism," she said, "and that whole thing."

Quinta stood in the middle of the living room floor. She didn't have to move any furniture, because there was hardly any at all. She asked:

"Is there anything you want to say?"

Lucas shrugged. "I don't . . ."

Quinta always felt some empathy for the people she worked on. It was a prerequisite for good results. Lucas Jameson was no exception. While she had waited for him to return, she had lain in his bed and read the books from his tasteful, though battered, collection. She wondered what kind of man he was to live alone in a once-elegant apartment like this. And what he had done to deserve what she was going to give him when he got back. She cracked her knuckles.

"A woman's got to do," said Quinta Mechanic, "what a woman's got to do."

* * *

Phyllis Lantern, in seat 32C, broke into a cold sweat. She was hemmed in by a fourteen-year-old boy and his mother, who was trying to fasten his seat belt.

"Let me do it myself," he protested.

When she looked out the window, she could see Jonathan. He was standing in the gate area, behind the smoky glass wall. Briefly he had waved to her, when she first sat down, but now he merely stood there smoking a cigarette. She had briefly considered exiting the airplane. Lucas was not among the passengers. It was too early for things to go wrong. Yet every time she looked over, she saw only Jonathan.

Did you turn the other cheek? No, I busted him in the chops. Everybody's got their little curse . . . my bad temper . . . sometimes can't control it . . .

And before she could decide anything, they had closed the doors. The plane—she glanced the nine seats across in this wide-bodied craft—was absurdly big to fly. She had not flown very much. She felt sick. She could hear the motor begin to hum, the foolish instructions from the loudspeakers, and the kid next to her entreating his mother:

"Leave me alone. Just leave me alone."

The plane was taxiing toward the runway. Phyllis could have used a little oxygen, the way she saw it. But the mask stayed in its little compartment. She glanced nervously at her ticket. New York to—

Boca Raton!

The stewardesses were all strapped in as the plane was readying to take off. Phyllis punched the emergency button anyway, and one of them came running. This one had small, sharp teeth.

"Isn't this plane flying to Palm Beach? West P—"

The stewardess shook her head. "No, this flight is to Boca Raton."

"Not Un—"

"American Flight 316," smiled the stewardess. "Did you buy the wrong ticket, honey?"

Phyllis nodded desperately.

"Well, don't worry about it now. Palm Beach is only about thirty miles from Boca Raton, and it'll be no trouble at all to arrange ground transportation once we reach our destination."

"Ground tr—"

"Now just enjoy the flight and, again, thanks for flying American!"

For a moment Phyllis refused to accept it. She remembered Jonathan saying *The plane's a little late* . . . She and Lucas had telephoned the airline, and Jonathan had confirmed a reservation for her on United Flight 409. The words of the airline bureaucrat spilled into her head. *Pick up your tickets at least one hour* . . .

West Palm Beach. Where the detective was waiting, in case Lucas couldn't make the flight. A good tail required two vehicles. At least one vehicle . . . Where the hell was Boca Raton? Thirty miles might as well have been thirty thousand.

As the plane left the ground, its take-off tugging at her stomach, the boy beside her leaned across her lap to gaze out the window. He was a light-haired child with freckles across the bridge of his nose. His mother pulled him back, but he wrenched free of her. He grinned at Phyllis.

"You think we're gonna crash?"

With trembling fingers Phyllis lit a cigarette just as the No Smoking sign went off. She inhaled deeply. "What's your name, kid?"

"Nathan."

"Well, Nathan," she whispered, looking down below, feeling her heart flutter. "Fuck you and your mother both."

SIXTEEN

The Verrazano Narrows Bridge, which connects Staten Island with Brooklyn at the neck of New York Bay, is the longest suspension bridge in the world today. As far as Quinta Mechanic was concerned, it had the Golden Gate beat all hollow. The steel cables, powerful and delicate, weaved harmony in the structure, while the magnificent towers took firm control of the graceful sag—there really was no comparison. Every time Quinta saw it, she felt the swell of aesthetic delight. It was no different this Wednesday morning, with clouds shimmering on the horizon, as she passed it on the Belt Parkway in her exhilarating drive south to the sea.

It had been a beautiful, exciting morning for Quinta Mechanic. And although she couldn't communicate it, as an artist might, on an enduring canvas, that didn't seem to matter. It was still work in the service of a muse, and Quinta was quite sure that she had brought beauty to its knees. She felt fine.

When Lucas Jameson had realized what was going to happen to him, he had acted very wisely, Quinta believed. He had tried to protect his face and teeth and had kept his hands curled into fists to keep her from breaking his fingers. It hadn't much mattered, of course, but it was the smartest thing to do.

Quinta also suspected that Lucas Jameson had suffered a concussion when his head bounced along the marble hallway. Certainly, as he lay now in the back seat of the car she was driving, he looked a mess. The upholstery didn't look too good, either. After the airplane spin, of course, he was unconscious. When she laid him out in the living room, she checked his pulse before she started breaking his bones.

Long before Lucas Jameson had had the bad luck to return to his apartment, Quinta had settled on the automobile she would steal. It belonged to an employee of the Public Theater who always arrived at work at eight in the morning. It was a late model Plymouth sedan and no more difficult to hot-wire than a bicycle. Its owner probably had theft insurance. It was a small sacrifice to make for art, anyway, and it drove like a dream.

Gravesend Bay seemed very aptly named that morning. Quinta followed the shoreline along the Belt Parkway to the exit at Stillwell Avenue. A couple of blocks further on she turned into Neptune Avenue. Then she was in Coney Island. Quinta Mechanic, who had grown up in nearby Brighton Beach, knew these streets like the back of her fist. However, she didn't think about her father, who was probably working out at the gym this very moment, nor did she dredge up any old, unpleasant memories. She left Neptune at Fifteenth Street and, as she passed Joe's Rooms, waved to the crockery flamingoes in the terrace garden. She drove down Surf Avenue to her destination, Funland. The gate was open, as she knew it would be, and although the place was empty of patrons this early in the morning in the pre-season, she knew she would find Eddie Waxer working on the Mouse, the double-tiered roller coaster that was eighty years old and more frightening than ever. She stopped the car and got out.

"Ho, Eddie!"

The man working on the tracks slipped through the frame and climbed down.

"I'll be goddamned."

Eddie Waxer was a squat fellow, just three feet, four inches tall. He had known Quinta since she was four months old and weighed twenty-eight pounds. He had been sorry when she passed four feet.

"How are you, Eddie?"

The little man grinned a toothless smile. "A little short."

"I've got a live one in the back seat."

Eddie stood on his toes and peered into the back window. "He don't look live to me."

"Yeah." Quinta nodded. "He had an accident."
She surveyed the park. "What's working?"

"Whaddaya mean, what's workin'? The park ain't
even open till Memorial Day."

Quinta smiled and reached into her shirt pocket.
She peeled off a hundred-dollar bill and handed it to
Eddie, who folded it twice and pressed it into a
pocket in his belt.

"So everything's workin'," he shrugged. "Every
damn thing but the old parachute drop."

"Forget that," said Quinta. She pointed to the big
ferris wheel. "What about that?"

"The Wonder Wheel? Okay by me."

They got into the car and drove to the ticket window.
Lucas Jameson didn't need a ticket. Eddie unlocked
the gate and on his thick ring found the key that
unlocked the motor. By the time he was ready to help
Quinta, she didn't need any. She carried Lucas onto
the landing and opened the door to a cage. She
deposited him inside and closed the door.

"He'll have a nice ride," said Quinta. "Take him
to the top."

Eddie started the wheel. Quinta looked back at the
car; she was going to have to do something with that.

"I dunno," said Eddie. "But there's a big wide
wonderful ocean out there. How about that?"

Quinta Mechanic looked out across the Atlantic.
She shrugged. That would do fine.

PART TWO

SEVENTEEN

The midafternoon sun filtered through the high, small rectangular windows. The air conditioner was humming steadily. The small portable television set was turned on, but the volume was off. On the screen spacemen were invading earth. Beside the television, on the long plastic coffee table which was coterminous with the foam cushion divan, was a stack of comic books devoted to science fiction. Next to them stood an open quart of milk and a box of cookies. On the divan lay the boy.

His name was Teddy. He was eleven years old. He was slender and fresh-skinned, a brown-eyed boy with auburn hair carefully combed in a wave. He had well-proportioned features, with a small, set mouth and an upturned nose.

He gazed blankly at the television before shutting his eyes.

My earthly name is Theodore Dray. I have come from the planet Quexquar. My father and mother are Emperor and Empress in the Land of Traskometichak. I have been sent on a desperate mission to earth to rescue their daughter, my sister the beautiful Elkezar, who has been abducted to satisfy the whims and wants of the as-yet uncrowned King of Albania, the most notorious nation-state in the Communist world. For many days my radio messages have been intercepted and my parents, who have no idea of my whereabouts, have been forced to state publicly that I am dead. Their weeping can be heard through the galaxies. Meanwhile, I have but forty-eight hours to retrieve my sister, who now hangs naked and bound with hemp from the ceiling of a small but well-stocked castle in the Albanian Alps.

Teddy's reverie was interrupted by the ringing of the telephone in the other room. He put his hands to his ears.

Fortunately, I have recently come under the protection of one of the most famous leaders of the underground, whose deeds for good are unequalled in all human civilization, whose advice and counsel I sorely need to vanquish the offenders of Peace and

*Justice. I mean, of course, the celebrated and re-
nowned General . . .*

The telephone was finally answered. Teddy uncov-
ered his ears and glanced at the television set, where
a commercial had interrupted the movie.

. . . Luis Barrezia!

Who answered the telephone. He had been sleeping.
It was still daylight. He could hear the muted sounds
of birds outside.

"I'm so glad you're up, Luis."

It was Sylvia Barnes. Barrezia smiled into the
mouthpiece. "Am always up. *Buenos tardes, Señora.*"
He raised himself up from the bed, and a shaft of
sunlight caught his eyes, which he shaded. "What
day today?"

"This is Thursday. I'm calling be—"

"Thursday very good day."

"Because that package you called me about, it
arrived yesterday."

"Very good. Jonathan—"

"He'll be back tonight." Sylvia paused. "Can you
wait just a minute, Luis?"

"I wait."

Barrezia rose and stretched, the telephone still at
his ear. A cardinal was perched on the baobab tree
just outside the trailer. Over the phone he heard a big
noise, like a door slamming.

"She's out now," said Sylvia, back on the line.

"Out cold?"

"That's right. It hasn't been easy, Luis."

"What? She give you trouble?"

"From the get-go. She sure has. And now she's
real sick."

"Oh—" He clucked sympathetically.

"I want you to take her off my hands," said Sylvia. "I don't want to wait for Jonathan to come back. She ruined my bougainvilleas, for one thing. I don't want to tell you what she called me, but it wasn't pretty. I just can't put up with this any more. I expect the girls that come through here to respect me, you know what I mean. I'm afraid I had to hit her, Luis. Even after I gave her the mashed up pills in the meat loaf. I don't like to hit anybody, you know me."

Barrezia frowned. "But still in one piece, yes?"

"So far, but I can't promise anything. Nothing puts her to sleep for very long. And I'm here all by myself, Luis. She called me some names I haven't heard in fifteen years."

"I come over soon," said Barrezia. "Is very *valuable* package, Sylvia. Be please careful."

"I will only—"

"I be over in one hour."

Barrezia hung up the phone. He raised himself on tiptoes to see through the window. The cardinal was foraging on the ground.

Luis Barrezia lived in a forty-foot Princess trailer on the outskirts of West Palm Beach. It was cramped and in many ways uncomfortable, but a man can get used to any place. There were two bedrooms, and the Cuban used one as an office. There was a living-dining room and a small kitchen. The trailer was paneled throughout in plastic mahogany, and the furniture was nondescript. After living in it for nearly eight years, it was still as anonymous as the day he had bought it. This he preferred.

"Buenos tardes, amigo." When he was dressed, Barrezia squeezed through the hallway into the living room. The boy lay on the divan. "Do you have some coffee?"

Teddy lay with his forearm across his eyes. He looked in his own way, the soul of despair. He said, "I have some milk."

"I make some coffee, then." As he passed into the kitchen, Barrezia ran a hand through the boy's hair. "You sleep as much as me," he joked.

"Oh, cut it out."

The Cuban ran some water in a saucepan and put it on the stove to boil. Smiling, he reprimanded the boy gently. "Now be nice, no?"

"Nice. Nice." Teddy reacted with annoyance. He switched off the television, then sat up and rubbed his eyes. *Be nice.* Luis was always telling him that. He didn't feel nice. Only for Luis's sake did he try. In a neutral tone he asked: "Who called?"

"No business of yours," said Barrezia shortly. "You wish coffee, too?"

"Okay. Yes, okay." As he watched Barrezia set out two cups, he thought *On that fateful afternoon, which I will long remember, General Barrezia invited me to his headquarters for coffee . . .*

The earthly Teddy Dray had left his hometown of Duluth, Iowa, almost a year ago. He came from a good family, and after his father stabbed his mother, she died. He was a Superior Court judge. He committed suicide. Teddy probably should have been happy in the foster home of his uncle, but he was not. His uncle was a policeman who liked to dress in women's clothes, and if propriety were to be observed, Teddy was an interference. Thankfully, the family priest,

Father Luciani, had known of the problem and stepped in to help the boy. That was the first time Teddy was kissed on the lips by any man other than his father.

When Father Luciani had tired of Teddy—and had grown annoyed, too, at the boy's churlish behavior and destructive habits—he sent him, in trade for another, to a summer camp for Catholic boys. In a sense, that summer had never ended. In September Teddy had been borne off by a young counselor. After he was raped in the Terminal Hotel in St. Louis, and left there bleeding and hungry, he was on his own. The counselor had whispered in his ear, *Have I committed a sin, Teddy? Let God decide.*

"Come sit down," said Luis Barrezia to Teddy. The Cuban was busy at the stove. "Bring the milk."

Teddy complied. He walked the few steps to the table with his idiosyncratic swagger. He was wearing jeans, a checked button-down shirt, and penny loafers. A camper's knife hung from a chain on his belt. He set the carton of milk on the table with unnecessary deliberation.

And said: "I don't want any sugar."

While thinking: *The General was always generous with the sugar and drank his coffee* con leche, *as he said.*

The route by which, two months ago, Teddy had come to live with Luis Barrezia was complex. It was a tangled sequence of men. After he had been fed by the police, who'd picked him up for loitering, the pederastic circuit had, it seemed, taken him all over the country. He'd spend a few days with one man and then be sent on to another. Sometimes he'd travel with more than one boy, and other times he'd go alone. Nobody seemed to want to keep him. He had a reputation as a troublemaker. He was handsome, but he didn't treat the fellows right. Some of them were old and he laughed at their infirmities. Others feigned interest in sports when all they wanted was to suck him, and he would tell them so.

Then, one day not long ago, Luis Barrezia had rescued him—or so it seemed to Teddy. If, instead, it had at first been merely the repayment in flesh of an old debt, that mattered no longer. Before then, Teddy had been living in the home of an aging Mafioso, who seemed to like to keep a few boys around. Teddy was one among three or four who lived in a chicken house, formerly the carriage house of an old residence in New Orleans. Barrezia came in one day and picked him immediately. Teddy thought he must have possessed some secret information.

"Milk, no?" Barrezia poured water into cups with instant Bustelo.

"Yes." Teddy smiled quietly; it might have been taken for a smirk.

"I must leave soon." The Cuban sat down, stirring his coffee. "But I be back soon."

Calmly, the General disclosed his plans . . .

One thing Teddy knew, and for certain, was that Luis Barrezia was not like the others. Even now, dressed in a wrinkled white suit, barefooted, and with his thin black tie slung around his neck, the Cuban had an easygoing warmth. He liked Teddy's company—itself a feat—but he never took advantage. He was not queer. Sometimes they engaged in a little horseplay, but there never came that moment when the older man looked at you with a sudden surge of lust, slipped his hand down your pants, touched your cheek, and asked *Does that feel all right?*

No; rather, Luis had plans for him. Teddy did not yet know what they were. He sipped his coffee and said quietly, almost obsequiously:

"All right."

Barrezia could often see into his mind, as he could now, when he laughed. "Don't be disappointed! *Pollo pequeño!* Your time will come."

"When?" Teddy wanted to know.

I explained to the General that I hoped he would consider me at his service . . .

"I have special mission for you," said Barrezia. "Haven't I told you before?"

Teddy nodded. "But it's been *forever—*"

"Don't talk like a woman!"

He felt his face flush. "Yes," he said simply, correcting himself. "But you weren't specific."

"It will be a few weeks," said Barrezia. He sucked on his coffee as he stared at the boy. Who had been, it was true, confined to the trailer for quite some time. The loyalty was, after all, emerging. With a boy somewhat older it would have been a little easier. But young Teddy had all the earmarks of an excellent shotgun boy. In his hatred of everything which existed, save expediency, he reminded Barrezia of himself as a youth. Although Jonathan had not yet met him, he would be pleased. He supposed, in sum, that he could say:

"If you wish to come with me tonight, you may."

Teddy drank his coffee.

The General begged me to undertake this mission . . .

EIGHTEEN

Once she had called Luis, Sylvia Barnes felt much better. An hour gave her time to do her exercises and to take a bath. The girl had been really disruptive to her whole routine. Upstairs, outside the door to the girl's room, Sylvia listened for a moment. Phyllis was still moaning something terrible. Sylvia smiled with satisfaction and put a hand on the knob. She considered going in to comfort her some more, but then decided against it. The girl was filled with spite; it served her right. She shook her head.

"Poor thing."

Sylvia did not know *exactly* why Phyllis Lantern was in the guest bedroom. It had something to do with prostitution. She didn't know the particulars or why it was necessary to drug the girls. But it was Jonathan who sent them, and usually it was Jonathan who took them away. He made more money now than he ever did teaching math, and over all he was home more, too.

"It's business," he told her. He didn't need to add that it was best for her not to know any more. And for Sylvia it was pin money. For every girl who passed through her house, Jonathan gave her one hundred dollars to bet on the dogs.

In her bedroom Sylvia disrobed. The girl's moaning was audible until she shut her door. At fifty-four, Sylvia still had a respectable body. It pleased her to watch it while she exercised before the full-sized mirrors that covered the closet doors. Her breasts sagged slightly, and she had been unable to forestall a few facial wrinkles, but her belly was flat and her firm bottom rested on solid, thick thighs. She was a dancer. She lay down on the shag rug. Raising her hips and supporting her lower back with her hands, she began the bicycle pedaling exercise.

More important than the Cadillac Seville or her jewelry—both testaments to Jonathan's material success in the world—was Sylvia's sense of pride and accomplishment at having been a good mother to her son.

"Jonathan does all right," she would say to her weekly bridge club.

"Yes," Esther, Wilma or Elizabeth might ask, "but what does he do?"

"He takes care of me."

This response excited the envy of her friends. It had also engendered the belief that Jonathan was somehow involved in the mob. Sylvia knew that was unfounded, although Andrea Grotstein, whose son almost certainly was a gangster, said the same thing:

"Jimmy takes care of me."

Sylvia's good luck with her son was a continuation, she felt, of the lucky stars that had guided her all her life. She was a Taurus, born early in May, with her moon in Aries. It was the kind of sign that got you what you wanted. Sylvia had come from Georgia. Her relatives worked in the turpentine woods; her parents were poor white tenant farmers. Sylvia was one of ten children. At fourteen, just after World War II brought her brothers home to roost, Sylvia had struck out on her own.

She could dance—or so she found out when she reached St. Pete—and it wasn't long before she was working the torrid county fair circuit. In the winters she worked as a stripper in the night clubs along Biscayne Boulevard in Miami.

After she had pedaled in the air for a few minutes, Sylvia assumed a natal-like position, with her knees drawn up. She began to roll from one side to the other. She had long dispensed with the exercise record, but she could still hear the voice of the sturdy Jack La Lanne. *One and two and one and . . .*

In 1947 one of Sylvia's boy friends taught her to drive. She wanted to buy a car to show her family in Georgia for Christmas. She made a pornographic movie. An Orthodox rabbi named Hiram Schiffin was paying girls fifty dollars an afternoon for shooting stag films.

"Twenty now," said Hiram, when she got to the Flager Motel, "thirty later." He was a lewd rabbi, but he was well known for his circumspect behavior with the actresses. Freddy Peaches, the other stag film maker in Miami, paid only forty dollars and tried to screw you himself.

In the first scenes that Hiram shot, Sylvia undressed seductively with all the wiles of a good stripteaser. Hiram told her to look at the camera like it was a man's eye.

"Very good," he said when it was over. "Now coffee and danish—and then Wilbur."

Wilbur was a muscular little dynamo who had taken a long bath especially for the occasion. Despite herself, Sylvia became frightened. She held back tears when Hiram asked her, please, to suck Wilbur's penis, which had a triangular purple head. But ultimately she let Wilbur kiss her breasts, and french her a little, and then poke her, first the regular way and afterwards from behind. After a while they stopped. Relieved, Sylvia drank more coffee and ate another danish.

"Let's go," said Hiram then. "Let's finish up now." It was almost sundown on a Friday.

"I thought we were finished," said Sylvia.

"I must get come shot."

So Wilbur had perforce mounted Sylvia once more on the same grimy sheets in the wobbly bed in the Flager Motel in South Miami on a rainy afternoon. Wilbur held her by the calves and pumped her. She watched his face turn red, and when he was about to ejaculate, he said so.

"Come shot!" shouted Hiram. Delighted, he brought the camera in tight on Sylvia's belly.

When Sylvia felt Wilbur begin to draw out of her, she wrestled her thighs around his back and drew him down. Why was he trying to get out of her? What was screwing for, anyway, but to feel the guy's juice shoot off inside you? Her dancer's thighs and calves were like a vise. Wilbur came tumbling down, and Sylvia rocked her bottom.

"You ruined it!" shouted Hiram. "You spoiled it!"

Jonathan Barnes issued from that union. Hiram Shiffin, although he was upset, paid her the thirty because he was honest and just.

Today Wilbur was a policeman in nearby Delray Beach. He knew that Jonathan was his son, although he never acknowledged it. He had a wife and four children. Sylvia had never asked him for one red cent. Sometimes, though, she gave him a call.

"Why don't you meet me at the airport, Will? I'm picking up a package this morning."

For her final exercise, Sylvia ran in place for three minutes. Then she took a bath. With the water running, she couldn't hear the girl moaning.

She was naked under the sheet. The woman had undressed her while she was passed out. Now she frequently had the shivers. Her mouth was dry. The bedroom door was locked; the room was windowless. When she tried to walk, she felt dizzy.

But she was not nearly as sick as she sounded. Her moans had become a habit; they covered her memory of what had happened. She remembered the airplane. She recalled disembarking. She felt like a spacewoman and was ready to abort the mission. She planned to find a cop. And telephone Lucas. And—

"Phyllis Lantern!" A hand had reached out for her as she walked into the terminal. The woman had red hair with the black roots showing. "Aren't you Phyllis, honey?"

"No."

Phyllis tried to wrench free. The woman ignored her efforts to break past. Sylvia Barnes was a big woman.

"Phyllis, meet an old friend of mine . . ."

She looked into the eyes of a cop.

"Will Harris. He's with the Delray Beach P.D."

She had decided in an instant to be polite. She smiled at Sylvia and at the cop. "I have to pick up my bag."

"That's fine, honey."

The cop didn't go away. They waited with her in the baggage claim.

The cop said, "That's a big bag." And took it from her.

"Wouldn't you know," Sylvia said to Phyllis, taking her arm, "my car's in the shop. If it weren't for Will here, I don't know how I would've met you."

"I'll drive you back home," said Will. He was a short, muscular cop with lazy, long eyelashes.

"This is just like being a teenager when I was arrested for shoplifting," joked Sylvia in the back of Will's iron grey automobile.

"I won't turn on the siren this time," said Will.

"It was just a damned hairbrush," said Sylvia, laughing, her freckled hand falling across Phyllis's lap. The woman squeezed her knee familiarly. "Didn't cost but fifty cents."

Phyllis had sat there in a murderous sweat and laughed artificially. She'd had some glimmer of hope that somehow Lucas or a detective was behind them. The woman's hand on her thigh was like an epoxy bond.

"You haven't ever been to Florida before, have you, Phyllis?"

"No."

Sylvia leaned forward. "We should slow down and show off the old landscape, shouldn't we, Will? What do they call those trees, anyway? I don't mean the palms; I mean the other ones."

"Coconut?" Will shrugged. "I'm not sure."

"Well, they're beautiful, aren't they?"

It gave Phyllis a chance to look out the window and see nothing, and say, "They really are."

By the time they had got "home" it was eleven-thirty in the morning. The moments after that receded, in memory, into an orgy of despair. Phyllis had no idea what to do. The cop had decided to stay for lunch. Phyllis remembered looking at the fresh red ground meat, the egg, the bread crumbs, the green pepper—all in a clear glass bowl—and thinking *Oh my god*. She recalled trying to wander out the kitchen door, but it was locked.

"Oh, I have to keep it locked, honey. This world ain't what it used to be. I got the air conditioner going, too. Here, you want to dice some raw onions? Now sit still, Will Harris. With this new oven Jonathan bought me, it just takes ten minutes to cook a whole meat loaf."

The woman was always touching and poking her, once even saying, "I can't keep my hands to myself, can I?" This led the cop to let out a big guffaw.

"What's the matter with you, Will Harris? You used to have the rovingest hands I ever met. Look at him laugh, Phyllis. Us dancers have to stick together." She patted Phyllis on the backside.

The lunch itself had died in her memory. *Here let me give you the end piece, darling.* She thought she had become dizzy before blacking out, but she couldn't say for sure. She also remembered the words: *That damn airplane food they serve. Take her legs, Will. Give her a chance to walk, Syl. Take her legs, damn you.*

She also had the vaguest visual memory of what she thought was the cop unbuckling his holster. She could have sworn it. It was the first thing to come back to her when she had come to dizzy consciousness. And then, with the pain, with her nakedness beneath the sweaty sheets, she knew also that she'd been raped.

It was that, feeling violated, which had so enraged her. She'd pounded on the door with her fists until they were raw. She'd screamed. In her ranting she had even found the used condom on the floor. She tried to stuff it in Sylvia's mouth when the woman finally came through the door: *What's the matter in here?* She had almost shoved it in her mouth; then the woman had slapped her once, viciously, on the side of the head. She was still weak, and suddenly dizzy again. The woman was screaming at her, sitting on her. They were on the floor. Sylvia was forcing both of Phyllis's arms beneath her own knees.

For the briefest moment they were quiet together, and sweat from Sylvia's forehead was dripping into Phyllis's eyes.

"I'm not supposed to hurt you," whispered Sylvia venemously. "But don't try my patience."

The pill had come into her hand like magic, and she forced it between Phyllis's lips. The woman seemed to think she was a cat and massaged her throat. Phyllis held the pill below her tongue, but she ceased struggling. Sylvia smiled.

"Now if you'll excuse me," she said, "I'm on the telephone."

Phyllis Lantern made one more effort to escape. It was when the big Cuban, whom she later came to know as the Piper, entered the room. He squeezed through the doorway with Sylvia, who had changed clothes and was now dressed in pleated corduroy trousers and a moss green blouse that showed a freckled cleavage.

"I guess I still know how to dress," she was giggling.

"*No necesito un sosten,*" grinned the Piper.

"Now don't talk Spanish," blushed Sylvia. "You know I don't understand it."

They were standing over her. Her eyes had fluttered open as they had come in, but she had shut them again.

"I brought Dr. Luis," said Sylvia, who reached down and gripped one of her legs. "Come on, I know you're awake."

"Eyes closed," observed Barrezia. "How are we today afternoon, little one?"

When Phyllis didn't respond, Sylvia said crossly, "She's been a little witch, Luis."

Barrezia sat down on the bed. He placed a hand on Phyllis's forehead and opened one eye with his thumb. "Sylvia offers Southern hospitality, does she not?"

Phyllis grimaced. She slivered open her eyes when Barrezia withdrew his hand. "Oh yeah," she said weakly.

"See what I mean?" asked Sylvia. "Dr. Luis is only trying to help."

She saw them both—his face close, drooping, and Sylvia's hovering behind his back. She noticed, too, his hand dipping into the pocket of his white jacket. It stayed there, the fingers working cleverly. Phyllis could imagine the syringe, could almost see the plastic sheath coming off the needle. Like she had X-ray vision. When he brought out his hand, it was closed in his fist.

Phyllis looked up at Sylvia and tried to smile. She whispered pathetically, "I'm afraid of doctors."

"Oh, honey." Sylvia responded to this childlike tone with renewed affection. "He's only here to help you."

Phyllis smiled bravely. She said loud and clear, "Then why don't you get your tits out of his face, you fucking cow—"

"Stick her, Luis—"

Phyllis snapped the sheet and shoved him violently, low, down near his hip, with her hands. He dropped off the bed like lead. She brought the sheet down and off her and sprang up and ran. She raced right through Sylvia's hands. Sylvia screamed. Her scream would have shattered crystal.

Outside the room Phyllis met a staircase. She ran down the stairs to the front door. She unchained it. She turned the knobs on two other locks. Since when did they have a crime problem in Florida? It was going to be nice outside. She didn't care how hot. And she was going out naked, getting extremely immodest in her old age. The front door opened so swiftly she was amazed.

But not the screen door. That was locked by one of those thingamajigs beneath the handle that you could never figure out which way it went. It went the other way. Phyllis tried it. Both ways. Then she got some help. A rough hand on her shoulder swung her around.

"You *awful, awful—*"

Sylvia Barnes began slapping the girl hard, getting her on the right cheek coming and the left cheek going.

"Wait!"

Barrezia tumbled down the stairs. He still had the syringe with most of the Seconal still inside it. Sylvia doubled the girl over, and Barrezia found her buttocks and stuck in the needle.

"Fuck you," said Phyllis.

"Hit her again," said Barrezia.

Sylvia did. Phyllis felt blood in her nose. She held back tears until they started to mingle with the blood. The walls were alive with cries of all the mortal girls like her. She imagined a ship moving toward her in the night. A slave ship. Sleep.

"Good," said Barrezia. In the car he had a suppository of Matropinal that he would insert before she waked.

"She's getting blood on my floor," said Sylvia.

She had let Phyllis go to the polished cork floor all in a crumple. Phyllis was naked and bleeding upon it darkly.

"Good you wax it," said Barrezia.

"You have to wax cork," said Sylvia Barnes, "or else it stains."

NINETEEN

. . . Speeding through the newly discovered galaxy at almost the velocity of light, with no star map to guide us, the General and I were truly in a race against time, against death.

"Do you must pee?"

"No."

"Are you tired?"

"I'll be all right," said Teddy. He was tired, in fact, and he had to piss bad.

"I tell you it is long ride," said Barrezia.

"I don't care."

They had been on the road for more than six hours already. It was midnight. There was still a long way to go. They were traveling through the midsection of Florida. Half an hour ago they had passed Gainesville and Barrezia had left the main highway. They were driving along a dusty, buckling two-lane road. Trees lined the road; the horizon was lost. A slow-moving skunk got crushed beneath the car, and Teddy giggled. From all forward directions insects were hurled into the path of the windshield and died beneath the wipers. A small white sign flashed before them: SUWANEE CY, and Barrezia said:

"We come now to the pines."

The General informed me that we were quickly approaching our destination . . .

"You know what is a pine."

"Of course," said Teddy.

"This all once used to be pine land. Swamp, too. We go where it still is."

Teddy tried to stay awake. He felt that Luis was testing him, and it was important that he train both his mind and body. He did not ask unnecessary questions, just as he did not ask the Cuban to stop by the roadside so he could relieve himself. He knew they were headed into the piney woods of northern Florida, near the Georgia border. He suspected that the reason why lay with the girl who was unconscious in the back of the station wagon. Sometimes, when they went around a sharp turn or descended a rolling hill, he could hear her body roll a little. But he was certain that she was still alive because once in a while Luis asked him to check her breathing. She was still breathing. The blood had dried on her face.

"She American girl," confided Barrezia to Teddy. "They fetch very well price."

The General began to explain a little to me, his tight-wound voice crisp and intimate.

"They come food in bellies," Barrezia went on, "flesh no starved, eyes no redshot. No disease, no sickness, only sometime schizophrenia. You know what is schizophrenia?"

"Yeah," said Teddy. He looked down. It was what the doctors always said he had. Borderland schizophrenia.

"In Havana," said Barrezia, "it used to be different. We used to get little virgins from wealthy bourgeois families. They dance naked in cabarets. They say mass in morning, come dance at night."

"But that was long ago, you said."

"Oh, yes, is before revolution. Is 1950. Before you were born, before Castro, before whole world go to shreds." Barrezia smiled sadly. "There is no accounting for history. Is there . . ." He glanced in the rear view mirror. "Phyllis? History is unaccountable, isn't it?"

"She's not answering," said Teddy. He reached in the back and shook her.

"She has been especially hard," said Barrezia. "She must be correctly trained."

"I see what you mean," smirked Teddy.

"Is not easy."

"I guess not."

"We use many pills, much darkness, and the men are hung like they are horses."

"Uh-huh."

"State troopers."

"How long does it take?"

The Cuban cocked his head. "Oh, it depends. Every girl different." He smiled. "Believe it or not."

Teddy breathed, "I have to go."

But the Cuban reached across and laid a hand on the boy's knee. "And after they are trained: that is when you come in, *amigo!*"

Teddy closed his eyes against the pain in his groin. *The General gripped my shoulder. "Here, young Teddy, is where your expertise becomes invaluable!"*

They arrived at two in the morning. They could hear the dogs begin to bark as the headlights bounced along the rutted lane. At a white gate the Cuban stopped. He handed Teddy a key ring.

"Padlock on gate. Be no afraid, dogs are penned."

Teddy swung open the gate, and when he got back in the car, the Cuban smiled.

"Now: listen for cries of girls."

"I don't hear any," said Teddy. They drove slowly along the path.

"You are not supposed to." Every girl was locked in a hut which was supposed to be soundproofed. But this precaution was one of Barrezia's eccentricities, so far as the Drummonds were concerned. The Drummonds even liked the cries of the girls, and there was nobody else to hear them. Not for miles.

As they approached a small frame house set uneasily in a clearing, the lights went on. Soon enough an old man appeared on the porch, in a nightshirt, wiping sleep from his eyes. He shielded his eyes from the headlights.

"This man George Drummond," said Barrezia.

"He's old," commented Teddy.

"His son Woodrow have big pecker."

George Drummond and his son ran the training grounds for the Pipeline. For many years he had owned a turpentine camp and collected the gum from the slash pine that was used for pitch and resin and to make ships and paper pulp and railroad ties. Years ago he had sold all but a thousand acres to one of the big naval stores operations.

"A little late, Mr. Barrezia," noted George Drummond with a small smile. "A body can't get any sleep on your hours."

"Body?" Barrezia grinned. "I bring you body." He waited for the boy to come around the car and put an arm around his shoulder. "This Teddy, my *amigo*."

"How do you do, Mr. Teddy?" asked George Drummond politely. He turned his head and shouted: *"Woodrow!"*

In a moment Woodrow Drummond joined his father on the porch. Hitching up his jeans, he came out the door thick as an oak and nearly as tall. "Oh, howdy, Mr. Barrezia."

"They brought us a girl, Woodrow."

"Uh-huh." George slowly comprehended, and a smile dawned on his thick lips. "Shine?"

"No, a blonde. You must be very careful with her."

Woodrow nodded through his disappointment. He liked Negro girls the best, Spanish after that, and white girls last.

"Well, don't just stand there, son." George Drummond revealed that his teeth were not in. "Get a move on."

"She's in back," said Barrezia, pointing to the station wagon.

"Put her in number three," said the old man. "And use one of them new padlocks we bought."

Luis Barrezia smiled reassuringly at Teddy, who was following the whole operation with great interest. From his jacket pocket the Cuban withdrew a phial of the drug Trifanol. The phial had two hundred-dollar bills wrapped around it and secured with a rubber band. He tossed it to George. "Every six hours unless she have convulsions."

"You betcha," said the old man. "Yes, sir."

Teddy looked on as Woodrow Drummond pulled Phyllis Lantern out of the car. He ducked out from under Barrezia to go watch. She was still asleep, and the big fellow hoisted her over his shoulder. When he shut the tailgate, he saw Teddy and smiled.

"All in a night's work. I never seen you before." He patted the girl's rump. "Number three, I guess, old gal."

Teddy walked beside Woodrow. They approached a small, prefabricated hut of corrugated metal. Woodrow unlatched the door. He liked neighborly strangers.

"Mr. Barrezia made my Daddy build all these," he said. "You can't hear nothin' from the outside. I kinda like to hear the girls groanin', but Mr. Barrezia, he don't care for it *a-tall*."

Woodrow turned on a lamp protected by a wire mesh. The room was bare, except for an army cot and a jar of Vaseline. Phyllis was deposited on the bed. Woodrow took a length of electrical wire from his back pocket and bound her wrists, then tied them to the frame of the cot.

"See, my Daddy used to run this place as a

teppentime camp,'' he said, testing the tautness of
the wire. ''And he used convict labor all the time. He
knows all there is to know about prisoners.'' Woodrow glanced up smiling. ''That's why Mr. Barrezia
likes him so much.''

The girl lay with her arms above her head. She
was wound in a blood-stained sheet which Woodrow
began to unravel. When she was naked, he bunched
up the sheet and tossed it in a corner. He lamented,
''I wisht she were a nigger. You ever had nigger
pussy, boy?''

''No.'' Teddy shook his head.

''I guess I'm peculiar,'' said Woodrow, ''but I
like shine the best. Spanish is okay.'' He pointed to
Phyllis. ''You want some of this?''

''Not right now,'' said Teddy.

''Ted-dy!'' It was Barrezia calling. ''We must now
go!''

*I heard my two-way radio begin to bleep. It was
General Barrezia with an important communiqué!*

Phyllis Lantern came briefly to consciousness that first
night in the hut. A wave of nausea swept over her,
and she gouged her lip until it was bloody. She tried
to open her eyes. She could only *hear the mice in the
grandfather clock running up and down as it struck.
Hello? Hello? Is this Ph—? Phy—, said a small
brown bird, picking up a worm, My name is Lu—.
The worm had big black eyes. The bird stared
impassively. My nest is near, my nest is . . .*

''You can go first, Pa. Look here, she's real clean.''

''She is fit to eat.''

''Don't talk like that, Pa. Here, your pecker's
gettin' hard already. Where's that jelly?''

PART THREE

L'automne déjà!

—Rimbaud

TWENTY

The raid was a bust. He stayed for a few days longer, but he knew it was pointless in his heart. After the final filthy press conference when they admitted it, he filed his dispatch at the Miami bureau and left.

The airplane tossed in the clouds, and he couldn't recall when he had felt so *tight*—the euphemism for every emotion which disobeyed him and which he longed to deposit in the lap of the retired fireman who sat next to him. Perhaps there was quitting. There was jumping down. He put his feelings in a sack and dropped them from twenty thousand feet. Except for his rage, which he kept within.

"Mighty tumultuous evening, isn't she?" asked the old fireman.

"Yes, mighty."

Lucas Jameson arrived in New York on the last flight from Miami at one in the morning. It was autumn already.

His flesh was grey. His eyes were ringed and one of them had a caffeine twitch. He was disheveled. His legs felt rubbery and were giving him pain again. As he limped to the escalator, he massaged his calf. As he went down he got the nosebleed. The dark spots on the stainless steel somehow amused him. For months he had been getting them. What was a little blood? he wondered.

He had no baggage in check. Through the sliding exit doors came the chill October wind. He was not properly dressed, he thought. Who are you? he wondered. Where do you think you're going?

Outside the airport he grabbed a cab going to midtown.

Lucas had spent eight weeks in Florida. Prior to that he had been six weeks on crutches and two months in St. Vincent's Hospital, including three weeks in traction and four days in intensive care after the operation for the strangled intestine. Sunshine said she visited, as did Roscoe Gatling, but Lucas didn't remember, perhaps because his eyes were bandaged. On the day they had removed the bandages, the old woman, Louise Cole, was there, dressed in a sealskin coat and tapping her cane:

"It was the Piper."

He was often told, while he was recovering, that he was lucky to be alive. Sometimes he felt that way. But there was one wound, a mental one, which continued to plague him.

He had not found Phyllis.

To salve that insult, Lucas could have reminded himself—if ever he recovered a sunny spirit, and he doubted he ever would—that he had succeeded, for the time being, in virtually breaking the Pipeline. But even so, the balm was inadequate because the Piper, whom he now knew to be a Cuban named Luis Barrezia, had escaped. And Jonathan, whose last name he knew to be Barnes and who was sometimes referred to as the Piper's Cub, had also disappeared. According to the police in Florida, they had vanished from the face of the earth.

With the help of Gus Sagze, who had since taken his mother and inamorata on a long vacation, Lucas had been able to assemble enough information to trace Jonathan Barnes to his home in Boca Raton, Florida. He had linked him to the Cuban. And he had connected both men to a training ground—just as Louise had predicted—in northern Florida.

The investigation had been, in fact, eminently successful. The detective he had hired to help him even said that Lucas deserved a good citizen award. Perhaps he did. It was a concerned member of the press who had almost got his head shot off by the old man named George Drummond. And good citizen Lucas Jameson who had immediately alerted the police.

And they had blown it.

*   *   *

Once in Manhattan Lucas had the taxi stop at a radio station in midtown. In the newsroom he found a copy of the dispatch he had filed a few hours before. It was in a puddle of paper on the floor. It had been nicely edited.

Roscoe Gatling seemed to think that Louise Cole didn't play much any more, but when Lucas found her, she was at the piano. The Venus Lounge was almost empty, and the bartender was counting his invisible tips. Louise was not singing, but she was softly playing a slow drag. It made him shiver like a rattlesnake. She noticed him then. The bartender wordlessly poured him a Pernod. The cane, silent on its rubber tip, tapped across the bare floor. She extended a hand.

"Roscoe told me you were coming back soon," said Louise. "I didn't know tonight."

"I got—ah, disgusted."

"The news isn't getting any better, is it?"

"No."

He spread the dispatch on the bar. Louise knocked once on the wood and a pair of reading glasses was set in front of her, spawned by the bartender's ruddy fingers.

MIAMI BEACH FLA
OCT 21 1 AM (EST)
A STATEWIDE MANHUNT FOR TWO SUSPECTS ACCUSED OF OPERATING A BIZARRE CHILD PROSTITUTION RING HAS ENDED IN FAILURE, ACCORDING TO AUTHORITIES. POLICE CONCEDED TONIGHT THAT BOTH LUIS BARREZIA, 48, AND JON-

ATHAN BARNES, 36, "HAVE PROBABLY
LEFT THE STATE."

THE SEARCH FOR THE PAIR, SAID TO
BE THE CHIEF PROPRIETORS OF A PROSTI-
TUTION "PIPELINE," BEGAN LAST WEEK
FOLLOWING A POLICE RAID ON A SO-
CALLED "TRAINING GROUND" LOCATED
IN THE REMOTE PINEY WOODS AREA OF
NORTHERN FLORIDA. IN A MOVE WHICH
WAS CRITICIZED BY SOME OBSERVERS
AS PREMATURE, STATE AND LOCAL
AUTHORITIES ARRESTED THE RETIRED
OWNER OF A TURPENTINE CAMP ON
CHARGES OF MANSLAUGHTER, KIDNAP-
ING, AND RAPE. IN CUSTODY ARE GEORGE
DRUMMOND, 59, AND HIS SON, WOOD-
ROW WILSON DRUMMOND, 32.

POLICE FOUND FIVE GIRLS, AGED 9 TO
14, BEING HELD CAPTIVE IN CONDITIONS
DESCRIBED AS PRIMITIVE AND APPALL-
ING. THE RAID ALSO NETTED WEAP-
ONS AND A CACHE OF ILLEGAL PRE-
SCRIPTION DRUGS. SEVERAL GRAVESITES
WERE ALSO LOCATED AT THE SCENE,
BUT NO POSITIVE IDENTIFICATIONS OF
VICTIMS HAVE BEEN MADE.

"Gravesites," said Louise, marking the place with
her finger. "They always have a little cemetery to
show the girls what can happen to them."

"It was a little ways off in the woods," nodded
Lucas. "Wooden crosses and one grave open."

"Open and waiting," nodded Louise.

ACCORDING TO CRITICS, THE RAID ALERTED BARREZIA AND BARNES, WHO IMMEDIATELY TOOK STEPS TO DESTROY INCRIMINATING DOCUMENTS AND MATERIALS, AND TO WARN CLIENTS OF POTENTIAL DANGERS. IN ADDITION, LUIS BARREZIA, A CUBAN EX-PATRIATE, VANISHED FROM THE TRAILER CAMP IN WHICH HE HAD BEEN LIVING FOR SEVERAL YEARS, NEAR WEST PALM BEACH, FLA. HIS TRAILER WAS LATER FOUND BY POLICE, STRIPPED AND BURNED. BARNES HAS ALSO DISAPPEARED.

"A FAMILY MAN"
JONATHAN BARNES WAS KNOWN BY HIS NEIGHBORS, UNTIL A WEEK AGO, AS A "QUIET, WELL-LIKED FELLOW" AND A MODEL CITIZEN. HE LIVED WITH HIS MOTHER, SYLVIA BARNES, IN A COMFORTABLE TWO-BEDROOM HOME ALONG ONE OF THE SERPENTINE, SHADY AVENUES THAT CHARACTERIZE THE COMMUNITY OF BOCA RATON.

"It used to be a rich town," said Lucas, smiling. "They once called it *beaucoup rotten*."
"That was Mencken."
"Yes."

UNTIL HIS EARLY, UNEXPLAINED RETIREMENT SEVERAL YEARS AGO, BARNES TAUGHT HIGH SCHOOL MATHEMATICS. HE HAS NO POLICE RECORD AND HIS

MOTHER CALLED HIM "A FAMILY MAN,
A GOOD BOY." MRS BARNES IS SCHED-
ULED TO TESTIFY AT A GRAND JURY
HEARING EARLY IN NOVEMBER. AL-
THOUGH SOME SOURCES INSIST THAT
SHE IS INVOLVED IN HER SON'S ACTIVI-
TIES, THE STATE'S ATTORNEY GENERAL
HAS REFUSED TO COMMENT, AND SHE
HAS NOT BEEN CHARGED WITH ANY
CRIME.

"She's in it up to her neck," Lucas amplified.

"A SPECIALIZED PIPELINE"
ALTHOUGH ORGANIZED CHILD-PROS-
TITUTION AND PORNOGRAPHY RINGS
ARE NOT UNCOMMON, FOR SEVERAL
YEARS THERE HAVE BEEN RUMORS OF A
UNIQUE "PIPELINE" WHICH CATERS NA-
TIONWIDE TO PIMPS AND INDIVIDUAL PE-
DOPHILES WHO ARE ABLE TO PAY UP TO
$50,000 TO PURCHASE OR "LEASE" PRE-
OR BARELY PUBESCENT BOYS AND GIRLS.
THE CHILDREN ARE GUARANTEED TO
BE TRAINED, DOCILE AND WILLING TO
GRANT VARIOUS SEXUAL FAVORS WHILE
HELD IN VIRTUAL BONDAGE. ACCORDING
TO SOME INFORMANTS, THE "PIPELINE"
EMPLOYED THE UNUSUAL MEASURE OF
DISPENSING THE CHILDREN IN PAIRS, PRE-
SUMABLY TO REINFORCE ALLEGIANCE.

Louise finished the dispatch and pushed it away
from her. She picked up the snifter of cognac and

swallowed it at once. "This takes me way back," she said, with the alcohol still in her throat. The bartender poured another, and she drank that also. "But no sign of Phyllis?"

"None." He shook his head.

"What do those boys in the training camp say?"

"Nothing. I don't think they know one girl from another."

"Does the Piper connect you with Phyllis?"

"I hope not." Lucas finished his Pernod and got another. They were getting drunk together, it seemed.

Louise rolled her eyes. "Because if they do, she's dead."

He knew that. He shrugged at the irony. "I'm through with them now. The police are supposed to find them, not me. I don't care."

"You spoiled their fun."

"Thank you."

"You did a good job, far as it went."

"I only care about her," he said.

"So do they."

"I— What?"

"The hell with these snifters. Give me a glass, darlin'." She glanced up. "I suppose they want to put the lid on. Don't you?"

"I *had* thought of that," he acknowledged.

"Why did you stop?"

"It hurts too much."

"It can't hurt *that* much," said Louise Cole, raising her glass. "Not so much that it let your brain turn into a damned old piss-hole. Cheers, Mr. Jameson. That Pernod is a good anaesthetic for the *body,* but it ain't doin' much for your mind. Skim the milk off the top and forget about that teat. You better find the child before they stop looking.''

"I know," breathed Lucas. He was disgusted with himself tonight. As every night. "Because if they stop looking . . ."

"That's right," nodded the old woman. "Then the lid's on tight and you won't never find her."

TWENTY-ONE

On Saturday afternoons, when Nurse Stewart was off getting plowed by a GP in Danbury, Fritz would have the most fun. He would put on his gloves, then open the door to the basement and call down the stairwell. Then he would hurry back to the bedroom. In his robe he'd sit upon the bed, already showered and powdered. He'd remove his gloves. And when they entered, he'd put a finger to his lips, just so:

"Let me *guess*," he tittered, pointing to the little blonde girl. "Are *you* Teddy?"

"No."

"I'm Teddy," said the other, pointing a thumb at his chest.

"Why of course!" He laughed delightedly. "Then *you* must be . . ."

"Vera."

Then deliberately—today as on each marvelous Saturday—they began to undress.

Watching them, he said, "Please put your clothes on the chair."

His name was Fritz Elysis; the children knew him by his first name only. He was sixty years old, a paunchy man with thinned hair and a red pencil mustache. For a year he had been retired—so distressed had he been when his wife, poor thing, had died, that he no longer had much will to work. He still gazed up to the night sky sometimes to see where her star—*their* star—had been extinguished. For a few weeks he had felt as if his life were over, and perhaps it was still, at this juncture, replete with the past. But who was he to deny himself?

"I do so enjoy it," said Fritz to the air, as though apologizing to God.

The girl had dispensed with her dress and was wearing little else. The boy was carefully folding his jeans over the back of the chair.

"And you look so lovely today, both of you."

He liked hearing himself talk. Talking had been his profession. The bypass operation, as well as Tinka's death, had been responsible for his retirement. Fritz Elysis had been a radio personality. He had worked hard for many years and had no time for anything else. He was a financial newsman. His syndicated spots summarized the most important stock information three times every business day. They had been heard in over one hundred markets nationwide.

"This *is* Fritz," he said to the children, who now were naked as the day they were born.

This is *Fritz Elysis. Prices edged lower today on the New York Exchange after an early morning case of woe failed to inspire sympathy on the part of institutional investors. I'll be back in one minute to tell you why . . .*

Perhaps thirty years of that was long enough. Sometimes, however, he wondered if his voice—which he often imagined to be an entity separate and distinct from himself—could understand. Could it sympathize with the troubles—Tinka's premature passing, the agony of heart failure—that had made him retire?

"I used to be on radio," he announced to the children. "I suppose you know that."

"You told us," said Teddy.

"I did?"

He spread his arms and they naturally drew closer to him. They were so like porcelain dolls, yet their skin was flesh. They reminded him invariably of himself, as he had been before he became what he ultimately did become. His skin was afflicted with keratoses and a few liver spots, nothing to be proud of, he thought. But their flesh was smooth and warm and yet cool to the touch of his fingers. As they came within his folding arms, he kissed each one on the cheek, although the boy was clearly embarrassed. Teddy looked him straight in the eye and asked:

"Do you want to lie down?"

"Oh . . ." He was discomfited by any crudity,

repulsed by ugliness. That was, he felt, one of the reasons he adored children. Yet he said, doubtfully, "Perhaps."

"Let's take off his robe," said the boy.

"Children!"

He had always been eccentric, which seemed to be one of the reasons men enjoyed giving him stock tips. But Fritz liked people and things to be clean, because it was a filthy world to which he had given his life. Stocks, bonds, feces. As he had grown older, this tendency, once vague, had become more pronounced. He'd had a studio built in his home, so as not to have to put his lips close to the microphone that other men also used. When the financial papers arrived each morning, he sprayed them with a disinfectant. And the children—*the children must be shaved!*

They were taking off his robe. It was aggravating but also exciting. The boy undid the belt of his robe. The girl, with pink-grey cheeks so clean and fresh, helped pull the robe from his shoulders. Each lifted one of his arms. He became their accomplice as he lifted his legs in response to their ministrations, and lay down.

"See my fish?" asked Fritz, suppressing a giggle.

The children glanced up, but they were not curious. He had built into the ceiling above his bed a tropical fish tank, which he could watch before he went to sleep. There were some scientists who proposed it was relaxing to watch fish.

"Doctors recommend—"

Touching. The boy was *touching* his penis. *Teddy,* he wanted to plead for virtue yet for more. More. The boy anticipated him by taking it in his mouth.

Would it get hard? Yes, if he ceased to concentrate, if he forgot about the germs, if the girl—

"Vera, *please*—"

The girl kneeled beside him with her hands on his chest, her fingers worrying his nipples as though he, too, were a woman. Vera had small breasts and dull, troubled eyes and a small colorless mouth. On her wrist was a charming tattoo. They all had the same tattoo, it seemed. They were all named Vera. He wanted her to kiss him, but he was afraid to ask. He wanted her to press her dirty mouth to his, to force her tongue inside his mouth. He hoped she would do it of her own volition.

"Spread your legs," said the boy, nudging them apart.

"He is so . . . crude, Vera." Fritz smiled weakly. Yet he couldn't resist. It *was* getting hard, after all.

As he closed his eyes, he grasped the girl's wrists. Now she was putting her lips upon his nipples and rubbing his belly. *She did not understand.* But he did not see how he could ask her, much less demand, what he wanted. No: instead she was moving his hand to her vulva. Did she think he wanted *that?*

"You're good and hard," announced Teddy suddenly. "You want to fuck her?"

"Please . . . No." He was breathing hard now. "Later." The boy was unutterably direct.

"Okay." Teddy shrugged.

Yet he gathered his own resolve from the boy's brazen words. He pulled the girl to him, wrapped his hands around the back of her head, and put her face to his.

Don't make me say it!

For a brief moment she did not understand, and

Fritz thought all was lost, in vain. But suddenly she began to do it, to kiss him. She put her lips on his. She had soft, cool lips with small pieces of flaky skin. Her tongue invaded his mouth. He could feel the germs decaying, but he didn't care. In his throat the famous voice of Fritz Elysis made guttural, involuntary sounds. *I love you!* he wanted to say. *Kiss me forever!* Tears sprang to his eyes. Perhaps she liked him. Later on he might show her a photograph of his wife. "I like you," he could almost hear her say. "I like you, Fritz."

Savagely he pressed her mouth to his.

And then, at three o'clock in the afternoon, he heard that ticker sputter. What a shame! he thought vaguely, as he lay enraptured. He fit inside her like a glove. She sat astride him, naked and clean and impassive but for the movements of her hips and thighs. The boy held her hand, as though balancing an airplane. How his mother used to speak of Lindbergh! With what reverence she had watched the ticker-tape parade when the famous pilot returned from Paris. Lucky Lindy! The Flying Fool!

Fritz, too, was a pilot. He, too, had connections with the French. And when he died he would also have a ticker-tape parade. He was, in fact, dying right now. They had warned him. He had not listened. He managed to whisper:

"*Digitalis* . . ."

"Say you like him," said Teddy. "He's losing his hard-on."

"Look at his face," she observed.

"Are you sick?" asked Teddy.

He couldn't answer. The crowds were cheering all

along Broadway. The streams of ticker tape snowed upon him as he rode in the open car, and he looked up and waved and smiled to the lunchtime workers who peered out of office windows.

"I like you," she said uselessly. She bent her face over his and took his cheeks in her hands. His cock came out of her, and she felt Teddy trying to stuff it back in. "I like you, Fritz."

"He's real fucking sick," said Teddy. "Look, he can't even talk."

The girl got off him. His lips had been extremely cold and trembling these last few minutes. His eyelids were fluttering, his pupils staring.

"Sick fucker," said Teddy, disgusted. He climbed off the bed.

Now there was only the pain, radiating across his chest and down his left arm. He needed the digitalis, he thought. Perhaps he could rise. He placed his goggles over his eyes. *Contact.* He tried to get up. The propellers could not get going. *Contact.*

Yes, he would be flying alone to Paris. If he could get off the ground.

"Help him up," said Teddy to the girl. Teddy folded his arms and stepped back. The girl put out a hand and tried to pull him.

Contact. Was all he had ever wanted. In his life. He could feel his lips turning blue. It was a frosty morning on the airfield. He was naked. His heart was doing the Lindy Hop. The ticker tape was coming out of his mouth, reminding him of a long time ago, when as a youth he had stood beside a ticker-tape machine at Goldman Sachs. He raised a finger with an idea of recounting to the crowd his experience

when he landed at Le Bourget. They hoisted him on
their shoulders and bore him off.

Fritz Elysis has landed in Paris!

The headlines blazed even as his heart stopped.
The *Spirit of Fritz* in a nose dive, a spin. He could
hear that ticker sputter with the crowds roaring below.
Parisians! His mother would be proud. He could see
her in the crowd of well-wishers. Fritz, Fritz! they
were chanting—

"He's dead," said Teddy, squatting beside the
body, his ear at the colorless chest. "He croaked."

The girl stared. "A heart attack?" she mused. It
was a distant but somehow familiar scene. "You
only die once, right?"

Teddy glanced up. "Yes, Stupid."

"Don't call me Stupid," said the girl.

"Dead." Teddy frowned in annoyance.

She was gazing now at the tattoo on her wrist. She
added, "And don't call me Vera, either."

As Fritz Elysis, the old and soon forgotten radio
voice of finance, lay dead in his bedroom, Teddy
Dray began to rifle the drawers of his desk and
dresser, looking for money and valuables and whatever else caught his fancy. The bedroom was ex-
ceedingly clean. Into a small plastic laundry bag
meant for underwear, Teddy deposited a gold wristwatch, a signet ring and diamond pinky ring, a small
ivory elephant, and a wad of cash wrapped in
cellophane. It was a pleasure to look through the
drawers; they were so ripe with things to steal. For
Teddy it was an automatic reaction because the old
rodent was phfft! In another way it was a business of
global importance. *In my bag I placed the artifacts*

which I thought would be most useful to our scientists on Quexquar.

He turned to the girl and said, "I'm gonna try the rest of the house. You wanta come with?"

They were alone that afternoon. The house was empty, and only the dead man's nurse was due that evening.

"No." The girl shook her head.

"I'm hungry, too. Aren't you?"

"Just get out."

"Listen . . ." Teddy pasted a grin on his mouth and went over to the girl. He stood behind her as she kneeled by the body. "What's with you?"

"Nothing."

He swung the plastic bag so it tapped her on the head. "You better get a move on. We got to get outa here before Slipshit comes." They called the nurse Mrs. Slipshit because they could hear her crepe soles on the basement stairs when she came down to bring them dinner.

The girl said nothing.

"And then I got to call," said Teddy. He wanted her to look at him, see him as he saw himself in the mirror over the laminated dresser, one hand on his hip and all aswagger. "I was supposed to call already, anyway. I have to call the Piper."

"You just leave me alone," said the girl. She did not remember who she was, but it had occured to her, as she saw the old man dying, while he was still within her and death just beginning to play upon his lips, that she was not *Vera*. The name was not familiar.

And now that he was dead, she also began to doubt that she had spent all her life in Florida. She even recalled some vague, grey cityscape, the scar of a river, a feeling of hardness like a rock. She had lived elsewhere, it seemed. Tennessee? It did not seem right. New York? She gave up, for the moment, frustrated.

When Teddy left the room, she began slowly to dress. Each article of clothing, none of which seemed particularly familiar, she examined for some clue to who she was. Perhaps, she thought idly, she had been to summer camp. She gazed at herself for a long time in the mirror. The face and the body were her own, certainly. She toyed with various names, among them Phyllis. But none seemed right. She would have to think of something.

She began to wander through the house. Being with the dead man in the same room made her shiver. It was an expensive, elegant house; she had known that all along. She had no idea where it was located. Vague landscapes tumbled through her head. When she looked out the window it was apparent they were not quite in the country. Fields of high grass sprang up past a tended lawn, and the tops of other houses and smoke curling from chimneys could be seen in the distance. The house seemed, in fact, to be located along the crest of a hill.

In the kitchen she found the boy. Teddy. She was certain of his name. He was eating a chunk of cold roast beef and a glass of milk.

"You know where we are," she said blankly.

"Sure." He was still naked and held his penis in one hand while he ate with the other. He sat at the formica counter on a tall stool.

"Where?"

He laughed. "Connecticut. You asked me before."

"I did?" She opened the refrigerator.

He sighed in faint exasperation. "We've been living here for a month, Stupid."

"Don't call me that."

"Ever since we left Florida. You remember Florida, don't you?"

"Sure," she lied. "Of course."

"That's where we're going back to, maybe. See, in the newspaper I read that I'm supposed to call." Teddy licked his lips, remembering these words: BABY GRANDS FOR RENT CONTACT MR WHITE. He repeated, "I was supposed to call already. I expect we'll be going back."

"Going back . . ."

"I'd better call right now, s'matter of fact." Teddy reached for the telephone with smiling self-importance. "Call the Piper—"

"Wait," she said without thinking. She shut the refrigerator.

"There's no time," he said simply.

They were staring at one another across the counter. The telephone was between them on the wall. He thought that the girl had an odd look in her eye. She was older than he was, and nearly the same size, perhaps an inch taller, or less. She had never treated him with anything but remote deference all these weeks that they had been together. He was, *according to the General,* responsible for her life. That meant, Barrezia had whispered to him quite confidentially, out of earshot of all moles, that he could kill her if necessary. But she was very valuable and should not be abused any more than was imperative.

Yet now, as he gazed across twenty-four inches of formica below the kitchen cabinets, something about

her had changed. Perhaps it was time for her pills.
No. They no longer took pills, except for the
tranquilizers, and she and he had taken two each just
a few hours before.

"What's wrong with you?" he asked.

She stared at him like she was some kind of clock
ticking. "Don't . . . call."

"Don't talk to me like that," he said. He felt
suddenly conscious of his nakedness. He reached for
the telephone.

"Going back?"

"Don't scream," he was about to say, but by then
she had ripped his hand off the phone and was dragging him bodily across the formica. He was the one
yelling. She pulled him to her side and spilled him on
the floor. He landed on his back and tried to scram-
ble up.

"You mental—" He was about to call her a mental case.

She knocked him down and sat on him, flailing at
him with closed fists. He felt himself, against his
will, burst suddenly into tears. Blood spurted from
his nose like a fountain.

"Going back!" She was screaming at him hoarsely.
Half of what she said couldn't be understood. His
ears were pounding.

In the instant that she let up, almost in surprise that
she herself had done anything at all, he slid out from
under. He shoved aside the stools and went running,
slipping across the floor. She went after him. And
caught him. They both crashed into the wall. She
grabbed hold of his hair and that was the worst pain.
For a half-second, as she peeled back his head like a
banana, he saw her face upside down. Her eyes were

amazed, but her mouth was curled in some weird impossible rage. He didn't think she would do anything else. He tasted blood and tried to smile through it. But then she was plunging him headlong into the paneling, using his head like a battering ram. Again and again.

"Going back! Going back! Going back!"

He heard her chanting only in the distance. His ears were ringing with the sounds of the galaxies. And far away he felt her grab his testicles, then a hot sting of pain as she pulled him off his feet, turned him a few degrees, and sent him careening the length of the kitchen floor. He felt the cold tile floor beneath him as he tried to push himself up with his hands, and failed. His head sank; he watched the dark spot of blood spread beneath his nose and mouth.

A short eon later she was standing over him, kicking him gently with her toe. She said quietly:

"We're not going back."

Not that she knew where they were going, if not back. While Teddy lay unconscious, she tried to find out where they were now. In her anger she had rendered the kitchen telephone inoperable, so she went wandering through the house. The ceilings were peaked with wooden rafters, and the furniture was spare and modern. On a table, beside a spray can of disinfectant, she found a pile of newspapers. The address label on the *Wall Street Journal* read:

F ELYSIS
P O BOX 236
Bulls Bridge CT 54201

She continued to wander through the house aimlessly until she found another telephone. She dialed the operator.

"How far is Bulls Bridge?"

"From where?"

She thought for a moment. "From New York?"

"Oh," said the operator, as though shrugging, "from New York City, that is about a hundred miles."

She returned to the kitchen, where Teddy was starting to come to. She must have hurt him. She nudged his rib cage now.

"Come on. Get up. We're going."

"Go—"

"We're not going back," she said. "Come on."

She wouldn't let him out of her sight while they got ready to leave. She took him into the bathroom and bathed the wounds on his face, back, and neck. There was a half gallon jug of Listerine and a jar of sterile cotton. He was quite docile and groggy. She knew where he kept the Valium, but she got to them first and wouldn't give him any. He cried.

"Shut up," she told him.

The nurse was due back any minute, it seemed. She packed their things hurriedly into plastic bags stolen from the kitchen, and she took some food. She appropriated the things that Teddy had stolen, especially the cash. There was $500. As a token, she let him have the gold watch.

"What time is it?" she asked him.

The watch was too big for his wrist. "Ten to six."

In the bedroom, Fritz Elysis lay stone-dead. She noticed all the color had drained from him and his body had a bluish tinge.

"Sick fucker," said Teddy.

"Close the door."

They assembled at the front door. She carried two plastic bags and he, one. She touched his forehead.

"It's turning black," she said.

"Leave it alone."

Teddy was dressed in his usual blue jeans, button-down shirt and levi jacket. The girl wore almost the same thing, but she had on a pink sweater instead of a shirt. They had one change of clothes in the plastic bags.

"Let's go, you're gonna go," he said.

With that remark, she dropped her bags and, gripping the collar of his jacket, twisted it. She put her face close to his and spoke through her teeth:

"You do everything I tell you. If anybody asks, you're my brother. My name is—"

"Vera," he breathed.

She slapped him lightly. "Don't call me that. My name is—"

He smirked. "Don't you know your name is Phyllis?"

"It's not." Perhaps she was wrong.

"Yes—"

"Don't call me that," she said. Even if she was Phyllis, she didn't want anybody to know. "Call me . . . Sandy."

"That's stupid."

She hit him. "Say it."

"Sandy. Even if it is . . ."

Then they set out. Across the fields. It was growing quite dark, although the night promised to be starry.

It was cold. They walked toward the vague sounds of distant trucks.

Caught! Manacled by the vicious Dragon Woman who forced me to follow in her wanton path across the barren earth!

TWENTY-TWO

The news that Fritz Elysis was dead came as a shock
to both Jonathan Barnes and his friend Luis Barrezia.
They learned of it on Monday morning, October 23.
They were in New York; it was almost noon, and
Barrezia was still in bed.

"We send flowers," suggested the Cuban. "We
write letter of condolence."

"His wife's already dead."

"Then we address his cock." Barrezia framed one hand and began to write in the air.

Jonathan and Barrezia had been in New York for almost a week. It was the best place for them to conclude their business before leaving the country. They were staying at the old Lincoln Hotel, in its current incarnation called the Milford Plaza. Long in advance they had made plans if the Pipeline leaked. The boys knew the number and when to call. And every morning Jonathan journeyed to the Out-of-Town News Stand across Seventh Avenue and picked up newspapers from a dozen cities. Among them was a Connecticut paper, the *Stamford Courant*. In which, this morning, he had found the obituary of Fritz Elysis. It was tantalizingly incomplete.

Fritz Elysis, a radio personality since the 1950s, who specialized in stock market analysis and financial reporting until his retirement last year, died yesterday in his home near Bulls Bridge. The apparent cause of death was a heart attack, but the county coroner said that an autopsy is planned for later this week. Mr. Elysis, 60, was married to the late Tinka Elysis; the couple had no children.

"No children," sneered Jonathan.

"It should be big story spread all over top front page if children found," sniffed Barrezia. "But you never know in this country."

"No," agreed Jonathan. It couldn't be counted on. Police so often kept the names of juveniles out of the press for—it seemed today to Jonathan and the Cuban—

the most outlandish reasons. "We can only wait for Teddy to call."

"Which should have been yesterday, no?" Barrezia was upset with the boy.

"Yes." Jonathan sighed. He strained to remember all he could about the old man. "A nurse. He had a nurse taking care of him."

The Cuban picked the room service menu off the night table. "I need nurse, no?"

Jonathan shook his head. He hated to see his friend becoming lethargic again. "I'll have to squeeze what I can from her."

"Yes, you squeeze," smiled Barrezia. "Then we go, is mopped up, all done—no?"

Jonathan nodded, a little sadly. "Yes."

Jonathan and Barrezia had acted swiftly when the Pipeline had been disrupted. Word of the impending raid had come through Sylvia, via the Del Ray Beach policeman, Wilbur Harris.

"And Will says that if you got anything to do with that old turpentine camp up north, you better cut it off right away," said Sylvia.

"That's interesting, Mother. Thank you," said Jonathan. He was in his den. He glanced up at his catcher's mask. "Did Will happen to mention who was behind all this?"

"Oh, he said it was this nosey old journalist named Luckl—"

"Lucas Jameson?"

"That's it," said Sylvia. "You know him? Will says he's been sniffin' around for weeks and weeks and just now gave out what he was up to."

Thereafter, the very name Lucas Jameson made

Jonathan clench his teeth in anger. They should have bought him off directly, with money, or just snuffed him, rather than have had Quinta Mechanic hang him out to dry. But shouldn't a month in traction have drilled a little sense into his head? One had to live by instinct, like himself, Jonathan supposed, but you couldn't count upon others doing the same. The Cuban was philosophical.

"It must happen someday, no? Better now we have time to burn our tracks behind us."

That was true. The Pipeline had been operating for almost ten years, and it was unrealistic to expect that it could have gone on forever without interruption. The important thing was to disassemble it carefully so that it could be reopened when the time came. In particular, the trust and good will of pedophiles all over the United States had to be retained.

It had been, therefore, with a sense of both duty and sadness that Jonathan had left his mother's house that same day she told him about the raid. He incinerated the few papers that might be troublesome, checked the guest room for bloodstains, and packed his bag.

"I have to leave for a while, Mother," he told her. "I'll call you before I get out of the country."

There were tears in Sylvia's eyes. He didn't often kiss his mother, but he put his lips to hers now.

"But we'll be together again, won't we, Jonathan?"

"You'll hear from me," he nodded. "If the police come, you'll know what to do."

And what he could not expect her to do on account of maternal instinct, he spelled out for her carefully. The lawyer would tell her the rest.

Barrezia had picked him up that evening in the station wagon. They hauled the big trailer, which for

so long the Cuban had called home, to a deserted
stretch of beach. Together, over an open campfire,
they burned the records and logs after making the
necessary memorizations. It was a lovely, cool evening and a delicious fog spread across the Atlantic.
The Cuban had poured gallons of kerosene through
the trailer, joking:

"My little Princess is like Buddhist monk, no?"

Jonathan struck a match. They watched it go up in
flames. Later they got rid of the station wagon the
same way.

A business enterprise like the Pipeline was, in
some ways, so intangible, so evanescent. What was
left after these physical records were destroyed? Whom
had they hurt? Whom had they damaged? Was the
maker of a coat hanger—in the Cuban's favorite
example—responsible for its condition after someone
else had twisted it up in order to perform an abortion?

In their decade of service, Jonathan Barnes and
Luis Barrezia had abducted a total of about sixty girls
of all races and creeds and classes. They were equal
opportunity indenturers. There had been, in addition,
the same number of young boys, usually acquired
without coercion. A few of the children had come
from other countries, notably Mexico and Korea, but
the Pipeline specialized in young American girls,
white or black. In several cases the girls were pur-
veyed by their own parents, but both Jonathan and
Luis Barrezia preferred kidnapping.

Of these girls, twelve had died before their sexual
servitude could begin, and another half-dozen had
been killed later on, like "Vera," when they escaped
or proved intractable.

Pimps were the main buyers of the Pipeline girls,

and the average price was $30,000 in cash, almost
doubled on account of inflation. Young boys, although they did not hold the cash value of a girl—the
market was glutted—could be used in other ways. In
fact, the major innovation of the Pipeline, and a
prime reason for its high reputation, was the use to
which the boys were put.

"We are originators," Luis Barrezia often reminded
Jonathan, proudly, "of shotgun boy."

The Pipeline preferred its clients—urged them, often in strong terms—to accept a young boy as companion to the girl sold in any transaction. The girls
had various reactions to the long and arduous training.
Some became amnesiac and disoriented, while others
were conciliatory and needed only drugs and promises.
A few became outright schizophrenics, though some
were schizoid before they ever met the Piper or reached
Drummond's turpentine camp. But there was nothing
like a good psychopathic shotgun boy to keep these
girls performing at their best. Barrezia personally
trained these boys, from whom he won their loyalty
and, often, outright devotion. The first such boy that
Barrezia had trained, in 1974, still wrote the Cuban
letters from prison.

The most difficult, and rewarding, assignment of
young girls was not to pimps—who worked in a
world where a whole network of police, courts, and
peer pressures kept the system well-oiled—but to
individual pedophiles. Jonathan and Barrezia had in-
stituted an expensive operation not unlike the Book-
of-the-Month Club. For $60,000 per year, a pedophile
would be sent a boy and a girl every forty to sixty
days. He had to supply good living conditions and
some facade of foster care. If he damaged the chil-

dren irreparably or wanted to keep one of them for good, he paid a one-time charge of $50,000. Prices were high because the risks were greater, the girls exceptionally desirable, and the boys well-tuned.

Like Phyllis Lantern and Teddy Dray.

A few days after the well-publicized raid on Drummond's turpentine camp, there had appeared in the want-ad sections of over a dozen newspapers around the country this offer:

> BABY GRANDS FOR RENT
> EXC Condition Guaranteed
> U Carry Contact Mr. White
> PO Box 14 New Hope MS 53421

This was a message to every boy in Barrezia's charge to make a telephone call. The Cuban waited every evening, from four until eight, in the Film Center Bar, an establishment in Hell's Kitchen that offered private phone booths. All the conversations were fundamentally the same:

"When time gets hard and evil triumphs, what is the task of the good man?"

"To stay the course."

"When the young girl strays from true path, what is the course of the true gusano?

"To send her to heaven."

"If the gusano fails, where will we meet?"

"Vahalia!"

Unless there was some special problem, the conversations ended there. Barrezia added:

"I will not forget you."

But the communiqué ended their attachment. The boys were to do as they pleased. They were not to kill the girls, nor the pedophiles, nor themselves, without a compelling reason.

Since the ads had appeared, Luis Barrezia had received thirteen telephone calls. Many of the boys fought bravely their tears. But there were fourteen boys. One didn't call.

Teddy.

Later that same Monday, in the early afternoon, Jonathan Barnes made his way across 45th Street. The weather was cold and there was a mild drizzle. The street was crowded and screwed up by a big hotel that was being erected. Jonathan was always aggravated by walking in midtown. Today in particular, the colorful theater marquees seemed to speak to him in an obscure, epigrammatic language: *You Can't Take It With You; Dreamgirls; 'night, Mother*. Especially the latter marquee was pregnant, for Jonathan, with meaning. He had not spoken to Sylvia since he had left the house. She was probably being watched, and her telephone was probably tapped. He would try to call her—however elliptically he might have to speak—once before he left the country. It was strange the way he missed her when they were apart, while at the same time she annoyed him when they were together.

Jonathan went to the New York Public Library. Although he was not himself a voracious reader, it was an institution which he had to respect. He especially had high regard for its block-long shelf of telephone books in the main reading room. There were directories for nearly everywhere including Bulls Bridge, Connecticut. This he consulted. He might have called the newspaper, or even the police, but he was being extremely cautious. He copied the number of each of the professional nursing services. There were none in Bulls Bridge proper, but several in Danbury and the surrounding area. From a telephone booth near the men's room, he called them all.

"Hello, my senile mother lives in Bulls Bridge and she needs a practical nurse because my wife can't always be there—"

He got her name. He was so certain of it that he could afford to be more direct:

"Mrs. Stewart? Mrs. Sandra Stewart?"

"Y-yes."

"I want *you* to know: I've got the children."

"Who is this?"

"They want to see you, Mrs. Stewart."

"No . . . No, they couldn't."

Jonathan smiled into the telephone. "They miss you. They said you weren't very nice, but they miss you."

"No. They don't, you've got it wrong. Is this some kind of joke?"

"I hope you didn't hurt them."

The woman's voice was high and tremulous. *"Hurt* them? I never laid a hand on them."

"But he died—"

"I wasn't even there! I was out and I can prove it. I already told the police. When I got back, the kids were gone! What are you—"

Jonathan hung up the telephone.

Outside, the light rain continued and the wind was sharper. Under the darkening sky the lights of Times Square were brilliant and insistent. Jonathan felt good; he even felt relieved. When the old bastard had croaked, Teddy had done the right thing. He had left the house immediately and dragged the girl with him. For not calling the Piper right away, he could certainly be forgiven. Barrezia maintained that Teddy was particularly sharp. No doubt he would call, if not today, then tomorrow. Various problems could arise. The Piper understood; so did the Piper's Cub.

Light-headed, Jonathan walked all the way across 42nd Street to Eighth Avenue. As he passed along the rain-soaked street, he averted his eyes from the street hustlers and petty dope peddlers and would-be pimps and derelicts. They loitered beneath the wild movie theaters and outside the grungy food parlors. He passed the luggage shops and camera shops, the pornographic book stores, live sex houses and p—

And peepshows.

Jonathan began to walk faster. He had never been to a peep show. He had never seen a stag film. As he walked, he wished to collar a stranger and tell him: *No, no! I have never been to a peepshow! I have never seen a—*

Except once.

In college. He had attended Florida State. On a scholarship. He lived in a dormitory and worked as a bus boy. At night he studied. An anthropology professor had a collection. It was all a matter of research! He used to invite the boys over. Jonathan never went. Once he decided to go. He remembered the smoke-filtered light projected upon the screen and the smell of beer and wine. The first films were not dirty and he began to enjoy himself. He remembered the voices of his friends:

"O.K. Professor. Let's have something hot."

He joined the hilarity. *"Yeah, hot."*

The image flickered on the screen. He finished his

beer and popped open another. He was dazed. He had been watching the screen for two minutes before he realized—

"Look at her tits!"

"Is she gonna take the rest off?"

His mother was smiling at him and bouncing her tits in his face. She was turning around and bending over. The other boys thought it was great fun. Did they know who it was? No, no—

"Who's that dude?"

He closed his eyes. He wanted to keep them closed. He thought to himself very calmly, *She is sucking his cock.* It was Wilbur Harris. *Why is she doing this? Why do I have to watch?* He could not get up and leave, or the others would know. For the same reason he could not keep his eyes closed. Already one of the boys was knocking him:

"What's amatter Barnes? You sick?"

He watched as they coupled. Once the wave of nausea had passed—he watched. He put fingers casually to his ears so as not to hear their comments. But it was no good. It was his mother, after all.

"He's gonna come. Lookit him!"

"She's wrappin' him. Look at her ass rock!"

"Where's the fuckin' sperm?"

The boys were disgusted, in fact, when there was no come shot. In the last few seconds there was the image of the furiously pumping penis suddenly clamped tight, the testicles hanging, his mother's ass in the air—but that was all, save the final half-smiling, half-grimacing face of Sylvia Barnes as she raised her hand—

"She's giving the finger. Lookit that!"

Jonathan Barnes had never been to a peep show. He had never seen a stag film. He did not go to the movies. He was, technically speaking, a virgin.

TWENTY-THREE

On that same Monday afternoon, Phyllis Lantern and Teddy Dray missed Jonathan Barnes on 42nd Street by only about ten minutes.

After they had left Fritz Elysis dead in his bedroom, they had walked across an open field and had come about an hour later to a highway. It was only a few minutes before they got a ride with a truck driver who was on his way to Pittsfield, Massachusetts.

That was the wrong way to New York; it was the opposite direction. But the important thing had been to get away as quickly as possible.

The truck driver was about forty years old, a big, genial man with leathery skin and a wiry mustache. He had a wife, he said, and four children. He could tell that Teddy had been knocked around. He even joked:

"Did your sister do it?"

"She ain—"

"I didn't do it," said Phyllis.

"What's your name?" he smiled.

"Teddy."

The driver and Teddy left her pointedly out of their conversation. Apparently the trucker had been in Viet Nam and didn't like to talk about it. Phyllis monitored the conversation carefully while gazing out the window as darkness fell. She didn't even notice anything was wrong until they got to the truck stop. The driver parked off in the shadows. Suddenly she heard:

"Do you like to have your stomach kissed?"

"If you want a blow job, mister, it's five bucks."

Teddy was nudging her. She had been sleeping or in a daze, she didn't know which. He whispered to her, "Let me get this guy."

"Why don't you wait outside?" the driver asked her.

She was afraid to stand up to him. His tattoos made hers look like nothing. It was all she could do to say through gritted teeth, "Come out when you're finished."

She piled out of the truck with her plastic bags. Then she was near tears worrying that they would both drive off and leave her. Teddy was bad, but being alone would be worse. She could hear them inside the truck, and when she looked over to the cafe, she saw men inside eating and talking. Too many men. She stood in the shadows waiting, and out of the nearby bushes a striped cat came to wish her well. She thought to kick it away, but it leaned persistently against her legs. Its warmth helped restore her composure; when she gazed up again at the truck, it was with a set mouth and steel eyes.

Teddy came, finally, jumping out of the truck with a smirk on his face. "He gave me ten."

The truck ignited and drove off. She said, "Let's eat."

In the cafe the truckers paid them little attention, plastic bags and all. They had enough money to get anything they wanted, and Phyllis had steak. She cut the pieces with a serrated knife and popped them in her mouth. Casually she asked:

"Did he suck you or you suck him?"

"He sucked me."

She nodded. After dinner they went outside, and when they walked around the back, she grabbed him by the back of his neck and pushed his head into the brick wall. She put the steak knife to his throat.

"You don't talk to anybody. You don't blow anybody. You understand?"

He began to weep. "I—I didn't—"

"Can it," she hissed. "Don't talk to anybody but me. You're mine. You belong to me."

He nodded slightly, enough to feel the blade. His face had crumpled with tears. "You don't know what I'm thinking," he said. "You don't know—"

With which words she drew the knife away. She tossed it in the bushes. It was the first of several violent fluctuations of emotion she had for him. His tears made her angry, yet she felt him in her gut like a baby of her own. She swung him around to face her.

"Of course I don't know what you're thinking." She still pressed him tightly to the wall. "I just want you to *do* what I tell you."

"Sure," he smiled.

That night they slept in a culvert. The next day they made it to Pittsfield and stayed in the Greyhound station. Then it was Monday and they got the bus to New York.

Even when she tried to be nice to him, Teddy was always trying her patience. He wanted to know where they were going, and why. How was she to know? She hardly even knew who she was. She only wanted to go somewhere quiet and safe for a while. She wanted to think things out. She knew that Teddy had been supposed to call—call the Piper. That was, she knew, somehow like calling death. She might as well just kill herself as let him do that. She couldn't explain the violent feeling behind the thought. She also believed that people wanted to trace her or find her. She didn't know who, but there were eyes everywhere. At Port Authority Teddy picked up the flyer that lay on the floor, signed by the police: WE'RE MORE THAN MEETS THE EYE.

"Give me that," she said. And as they walked through the cavernous terminal she read: *We have eyes and ears you don't even know about.*

"There's a cop following us," said Teddy. "Don't look back."

That was the one thing Teddy was good for: Cops.

He seemed to have a sixth sense for plainclothesmen, and he knew what to do when they were approached.

They hurried toward the exits. Phyllis was afraid of policemen. It seemed that in the past they had molested or raped her. When she even looked at one, she could feel him in her groin.

When they got outside, she said to Teddy, "If you let the pigs fuck you, where will all of it end?"

Outside it was that rainy, windy afternoon. They had emerged on Eighth Avenue. They crossed the street and walked to the corner of 42nd. There, a small crowd had gathered. They were listening to religious gospel music. One small old woman was playing an electric organ and singing in a high, strong voice:

> Can't nobody hide!
> Can't nobody hide—
> From God!

—with such repetition that it annoyed Teddy, who tried to pull her away. But there was something about the black woman and her singing that suggested to Phyllis that she knew this woman. No: it couldn't be. But she *had* known someone like that. Who could it be?

> You can hide from your elders,
> But you can't hide from God!
> Can't nobody hide
> From God!

"Sandy!" he cried, getting her name right for once. "Let's go."

They continued to walk up Eighth Avenue. From the moment that she had emerged from Port Authority, Phyllis knew that this was an old and decaying city. Had she been in it before? She thought so. It was not the place where she had been born, but she had lived here. Then, just a block away, she saw the sign, in ornate letters:

TIMES SQUARE
Motor Hotel

And her heart jumped. She pulled Teddy along, and for a moment stood before the polished brass revolving doors.

"I've been here before," she said flatly, aloud.

"You?" Teddy said with a touch of the swagger. "You never were anywhere."

"Don't say that."

Yet the people who came through the doors were unfamiliar, even threatening. Still, she could recall many details. The hotel matchbooks in their baby blue covers, the tiny bars of Calgon soap. She had seen the rooms, too. The dark green bedspread, the hexagonal tiles on the bathroom floor.

"Why don't we go in then?"

"I—" She was afraid.

She could remember, somehow, the window on a high floor, and the breeze making the drapes whisper. She was turned away from a man, and yet she could see an indistinct face in her memory. Impulsively she pulled the boy close to her.

"Teddy—"

"What?" He pulled away, but she held on. Beside a plastic pine tree they talked.

"I can hear your heart beating," she smiled.

"So?"

"You'll feel better . . ." she faltered, and picked up the thread, "if you stay close to me."

She was embracing him awkwardly, and he still carried his wretched plastic bag. People were occasionally watching them.

"You hurt me before," he said.

"I had to." Gently she touched the bruise on his cheek. "Now you're scared of me."

"I am *not* scared."

"Okay," she said. "You just let me take you. I won't let anything happen."

Teddy gazed at her curiously. At times she seemed to have some special knowledge of his mind. Unfortunately, it felt good to have her hold him. Even if her blue eyes were wild. Sometimes it was necessary to consort with the enemy. *General, I have made contact with our arch—*

"Take me where?" he asked.

"Leave it to me." She picked up her bags. "Let's go."

For the first time in ever so long—perhaps years, she didn't know—Phyllis felt almost good. There was something grand in all this. Even while it was terrible to be chased by people you didn't know and all the time in pursuit of whatever past you once possessed, it was still fine to be walking these streets, alive and free. She was not from Florida. Her name was Phyllis, but nobody knew but her and Teddy and a few people she wanted to stay away from. Soon she would remember more. Had she been a dancer? A whore? A little girl? What had happened to her?

"Don't walk so fast," he complained.

They came upon Times Square. The great signs were enrapturing. The boy was crying again, but what matter?

"You're just hungry, aren't you, Teddy? We'll get something to eat. We can go—"

The Dragon Woman pulled me through the sparkling galaxy! She made me offers which I could not refuse!

TWENTY-FOUR

On the following day, Tuesday, the *Daily News* began to run a series of articles on sexual enslavement. They were written by Lucas Jameson, author of *A Flame for Charlie*. The first installment had a garish historical cast and quoted the once-famous commissioner of Boston police, General Bingham, who asked: *What becomes of them? Where do they go? Why do they go? Into whose hands do they fall?*

In their hotel room, Jonathan Barnes read the entire article aloud to Luis Barrezia, who lay in bed with his hands folded behind his back as he sucked a cigar. The Cuban listened intently.

" '. . . and the original term, white slavery, is obsolete. According to one probably apocryphal story, it was coined about the turn of the century when Clifford G. Roe, an assistant state's attorney in Illinois, was wandering in Chicago's notorious red-light district. He came upon a disheveled young prostitute, who passed him a note from her crib, which read: HELP ME—I AM HELD CAPTIVE AS A WHITE SLAVE.' "

They both laughed.

"We are in great tradition," said Barrezia.

"I didn't know all this," nodded Jonathan. He was, in fact, impressed with himself. He had always known that their work was important, but he had never fully considered their place in history, their role in a tradition. If it hadn't been just absurd, he would've liked to have clipped the article and sent it to Sylvia.

"What installment tomorrow?"

Jonathan glanced at a blurb at the end of the article. "The Path to Bondage."

"When do we come in?"

"Thursday: The Infamous Pipeline."

Barrezia puffed on his cigar. "By then we be in Paraguay."

Jonathan glanced up. "Let's hope."

"He will call today afternoon," said the Cuban. "I am sure."

Teddy still had not called. About the danger this presented they shared an apprehension beyond words.

The danger could not be calculated. An autopsy was being performed in Connecticut. Who could tell what they might find out? Fritz Elysis might have a police record for sodomy, pederasty, even rape. Teddy would not talk, perhaps, but what about the girl?

"Phyllis girl no memory," muttered the Cuban telegraphically. "Why do we worry?"

"I'd worry if they'd showed her a picture of my mother," said Jonathan.

"We kill her first."

"Well, of course."

The *Daily News* was Quinta Mechanic's favorite newspaper. She was a loyal reader of that venerable tabloid. When she was growing up in Brooklyn, it was still called "New York's Picture Newspaper" and was written in a style that any school girl could understand. Twenty-odd years later Quinta still felt she owed it. It had all the local news, too many ads, but a good sports section. It had everything that a newspaper ought, except brains, but for brains there was no paper in New York to which she could turn. So she read the *News*.

With some interest Quinta followed the articles on sexual bondage. She liked the way that Tuesday's article was slanted toward history, which was pretty rare for the *Daily News*, with all due respect. It made her check the byline.

"I know the guy that wrote this," she told her husband over breakfast.

Merrill had read the article, too. "You know Lucas Jameson?"

"I met him once." Quinta shrugged. "He was pretty well-read, I thought."

"He had a bad accident a few months back."
"So I heard."

Wednesday's installment, about the sorts of homes that produced children ripe for sexual enslavement, made Quinta recall her own past. Although she had long since forgiven her father for all the pain he caused her, she felt that, in a mild way, she also had been railroaded as an adolescent. She sympathized with a child's need to rebel and regretted that there didn't seem to be any good way to grow up in American society. It was the sort of thing that was depressing to contemplate, and for a long time that morning she stood by the chess table at the picture window overlooking Central Park. In her mind she visualized that mingling of violence and desire that Marcel Duchamp had painted in his *The Passage from the Virgin to the Bride*. In the afternoon, when Merrill returned from the gallery, she told him:

"They really ought to fix those people's wagon."
"Whose?"
"Those guys who twist up kid's desires."
"They really ought," agreed Merrill.
"It just shows what a screwed-up society this is."

Quinta Mechanic was herself a great admirer of the Marquis de Sade. She still kept *120 Days of Sodom* on her night table for bedtime reading. In her view, the divine Marquis was one of the most misunderstood men since Jesus Christ. Sade exposed crime, Quinta thought, in all its banality, while at the same time exalting it for its stand against petty convention and foolish conformity. The essence of civilization was crime; the one and the other formed a covenant that was at the fundament of this strange world. And to breach this covenant—as Quinta felt she tried to do, in her own small way—therein lay beauty, unmasked.

It was with these thoughts in mind that Quinta jogged on late Wednesday evening to the Park Lane Hotel to pick up the bulldog edition of the *Daily News*. She brought it home and opened it at the big table in the living room, where Merrill was planning how his gallery would hang an upcoming exhibition by Maplethorpe.

"This is the installment about the Pipeline," she said.

"I'll read it after you."

Quinta glanced down the page and began to read. It seemed that Lucas Jameson had outdone himself. The prose had great velocity, clarity; it was factual and detailed. There was even a p—

A picture.

This photo of Jonathan Barnes was taken this year in a Manhattan restaurant—

"What's the matter, dear?" asked Merrill.

"Nothing," she said absently. "I—I have to—"

The color drained from her face. Quinta Mechanic was not under any illusion about the kind of people she worked for. Murderers, mobsters, insurance scammers, indemnity freaks. Once the CIA had hired her, and she hadn't even known it until later, when she felt obliged to send the money to Chile.

Merrill placed the back of his hand on her forehead. "You might have a little fever."

"I'm going to lie down," said Quinta. "I'll see you later."

In the bedroom Quinta dug into her dresser drawer and removed a scrapbook. She found the matchbook cover with the name Lucas Jameson written on it. It was from a restaurant called the Stage Canteen. She telephoned that establishment.

"I'd like to make a reservation," she said. "Where are you located?"

"We're on 45th Street, just off Eighth Avenue," said the mild voice of a restaurateur. "Just off the lower lobby of the Milford Plaza Hotel."

"That's real nice."

"For how many, please?"

Quinta hung up the phone, then undressed for bed. She did forty pushups and lay down. She turned off the light, and for a while she tried to sleep. She could not. She lay in bed with her hands laced behind her neck.

Twisting up kid's desires. Just the way wrestling had twisted up her insides. Infertility, they called it.

She wanted to fix their wagon.

In a moment she was reaching for Sade at the bedside. She opened it at random.

"To begin with," said the Duc de Blangis, *"there's a bit of infamy which I simply must perform . . ."*

TWENTY-FIVE

Lucas Jameson heard from Roscoe Gatling. They made an appointment for Thursday evening. The homicide detective's office, at Midtown North, was a square box in frosted glass with a desk, a telephone and rolodex, a picture of Gatling's wife before her breakdown, and a menu from Salty Leo's. The only addition was a Sony Betamax. The room smelled of fish. Gatling was eating clams on the half-shell from a paper box.

"You want the juice?"

Lucas accepted the styrofoam cup. He had always liked clam juice. It had a lovely, briny taste.

"There was an autopsy in Connecticut," said Gatling. "There was a lot of sperm at the scene. If the police had warned him once, they told him a dozen times not to fuck with young kids, but he kept fucking with them anyway. We're still waiting for your girl friend's fingerprints from Rock Island."

"She's not my girl f—"

"Your girl friend's fingerprints," repeated Gatling.

The Third Homicide Zone was still not interested in runaway girls abducted by a mythical white slaver. But Roscoe Gatling liked the pornography associated with sudden death.

"First of all," said the detective, reaching into a basket on his desk, "here's a copy of the nurse's deposition."

I, Sandra Stewart, HEREBY DEPOSETH, SAYING: For approximately one year I worked as a nurse taking care of the late Fritz Elysis. I am a registered practical nurse in the State of Connecticut. He hired me as a live-in, because, according to what he told me, he needed constant care since his wife had died and he had had a heart attack. I was paid $350 a week and worked 5½ days with Fridays all day and Saturday afternoons free.

As for the children, once I started working, Mr. Elysis said that sometimes he had a couple of children staying with him as part of a foster care program. They lived in rooms in the basement. They had their own kitchen and bathroom facilities. I hardly saw them except when, after I shopped, I brought them food or when Mr. Elysis asked me to give them the leftovers of his dinner. There was sometimes one child, but most times two. I never questioned anything about this arrangement or thought it was strange.

Once, when I was asleep, I heard sounds coming from Mr. Elysis's room. Awakened, I went down the hall because I thought he might be taken ill. Through the door I heard him breathing heavily and mentioning the names of private parts, but when I knocked he sent me away. This was at night, and I was scared after that of losing my job.

The last children he had arrived about a month before he died. I never said anything to them besides hello. There was a little boy and a little girl. During the day they were quiet. Once Mr. Elysis asked me to fill a prescription which he said was for the boy's nerves. It was for the tranquilizer Valium, 10 milligrams.

On the day I came home and Mr. Elysis had expired, the children were gone. That was the reason I waited so long before calling the police. He was already dead. I was thinking the children might have been very frightened.

I solemnly swear that the above is true to the best of my knowledge and belief . . .

"But some of it's a lie," said Lucas.

"Most of it," averred Gatling. "They're still working on her in Danbury. She has a conviction for forgery, and a bank account with $20,000 that she

didn't get from cleaning up the old man's shit—do
you mind if I talk like this?''

"No."

"The old man's shit: he probably gave it to her for
the extra services. But we don't know if she was in
contact with the Pipeline.''

"Probably not." Lucas shrugged.

"So I suppose it was natural she wanted to destroy
the evidence; maybe that was part of their agreement.
She incinerated his whole fucking library." Gatling
pointed over Lucas's head. "Lights?"

Lucas reached behind him and switched off the
lights. "She forgot one thing."

Gatling nodded. "She forgot the tape that was in
the machine."

Fritz Elysis had videotaped his own death. Gatling
pressed the button on the Betamax and turned on the
television set. The screen came alive with a burst of
light.

"The camera was in this fish tank he had above
his bed," explained Gatling.

"Fish tank?"

"Tropical fish. These screwy bastards'll do anything to relax. What's the matter, you don't like
fish?''

At first the screen was fuzzy and the images like
shadows.

"You can't see anything until he turns on the top
lights. You can see his hand reaching for the switch
now."

Indeed—the arm of the shadow straightened out,
and almost instantly the picture came into focus.
Gatling glanced at Lucas.

"Is it her?"

Lucas leaned forward. "I can't tell yet."

The man lay naked on the bed. His face was slightly flushed and a nervous smile could be detected on his lips. The children kneeled beside him. The boy was stroking his penis like it was a pet alligator. Then he put his head down and took it in his mouth. The girl was bending forward, ready to kiss his nipples, as she rubbed his stomach. Gatling leaned forward with his finger on the Betamax. For a brief second she raised her head and brushed back her hair. Gatling froze the image.

"Tell me."

"It's her."

There wasn't a shadow of a doubt. There were welts still healing on her back. Her complexion was grey, and her stare was . . . it was awful. And it was Phyllis.

"Feel better?" asked Gatling.

In fact, he felt relieved.

"She's alive, more or less," said Gatling.

He felt the relief extend through his entire body. The smell of the clam juice was still in his gullet. He wiped his eyes. "Her look," he said in a low voice.

"We can come back to it," said Gatling. He unfroze the tape.

As the boy pushed apart the old man's legs and positioned himself between them, Lucas commented, "He's getting his erection."

"It gets hot," agreed Gatling. "You sure you want to see the rest of it?"

"No." Lucas shook his head. "But I deserve it."

Gatling lit a cigarette. "It lasts about half an hour," he said matter-of-factly. "You'll like the last part."

TWENTY-SIX

There had been too many police in Manhattan for Phyllis and Teddy. They seemed to be swarming through Times Square; it was hard to turn around without seeing another one, plainclothesed or dressed in blue, eyeing them with lazy suspicion. As they ate hot dogs at Nathan's, Phyllis kept seeing the words CONEY ISLAND. She saw them again at the entrance to a subway. She had some vague recollection of any uneasy landscape that was somehow safe for children. They took the F train to the end of the line.

And it seemed to have been a good idea: on Coney Island there were not many cops. Phyllis and Teddy walked along the boardwalk beside the old amusement park. Most of the rides were closed for the season, but a few places were still open. It was easy to divert Teddy with the shooting galleries, the hoop games, and the bumping cars. That afternoon, at a pet store, he also wanted some goldfish, and she let him pick out two. The clerk put them in a plastic bag and sold them some food. It was another thing to carry.

The neighborhood beyond the amusement park was old and rundown. It was past dark by the time they went looking for a place to stay.

"The fish are going to die, aren't they?" asked Teddy.

"We have to get them in water," she agreed.

They finally found a place past Neptune Avenue, on 15th Street. It was an old, creaky boarding house. An Italian woman, her body thick and squat, her gums brown and rotting, asked no questions. Her name was DiMaggio.

She told Phyllis, "Hundred dollar a week."

She wanted the money in advance and hungrily eyed the roll of bills that Phyllis produced. "Bathroom in hall. No loud noise."

The room was small and dingy, with crooked walls and a linoleum floor, and one dirty window. There was a Murphy bed with sharp metal edges and broken springs. In the kitchenette was a hot plate and a refrigerator stocked with a pound of rotten meat. It must have been there for weeks. Teddy dropped it on the floor by mistake and a hundred filthy white, eyeless slugs began to roll across the floor. They were slimy and had no legs. It was an hour before Phyllis could get them cleaned up.

"They're alive," said Teddy. "They're like worms." He picked one up and wanted to put it in his mouth. She knocked it out of his hand. "I was just kidding."

One of the goldfish died before it found its new home in a bowl of water. Teddy overfed the survivor and named it Walter, after his father. He stared at it constantly for a couple of days, until they bought a television set. It was a small portable model that cost $110. Since it was on sale, with the money they saved, Phyllis bought Teddy a load of comic books. Thereafter the TV set was always on, and Teddy was always reading or lying down, and the fish grew fat in the porcelain bowl.

Although he knew that he was supposed to call the Piper, that his orders were clear, direct, and no less important to obey than the hand of God, Teddy could not seem to get a chance to do it. The days went past. Whenever Teddy saw a telephone, he pictured in his mind the smiling, brotherly face of Luis Barrezia.

But the girl was always with him. One afternoon, while they were out walking, he saw it was four o'clock and tried to sneak away. But he hadn't even put the dime in the slot before she was hitting him.

Teddy was not afraid of her. He was not afraid of anything. When Phyllis took him to the Coney Island Wax Museum he was particularly not frightened. He ate his popcorn and gazed impassively into the exhibits, which were tableaus of famous crimes. Ruth Snyder and Judd Gray, the nurse-killer Richard Speck. Teddy laughed at the sight of Fred Thompson, who had raped and killed a four-year-old girl. But his favorite scene was of Julio Ramirez Perez, who had killed a housewife with a screwdriver.

"Do you think it hurt?" he asked Phyllis.

She nodded.

"Is that what you were going to do to me?"

Phyllis grasped his hand.

"I mean, when you put the knife to my throat."

"I was mad, that's all." She put an arm around his shoulder. He edged away.

"Mad." That's what his father had said later, too. "You could put a screwdriver in me, too. I wouldn't cry."

"No."

"I wonder how it feels," he said. He remembered his mother bleeding on the kitchen floor. Before she died she said it hurt. To Phyllis, Teddy added: "If you want to try it on me, it's okay."

She tried to hold him. "I don't want to. Don't you know I don't?"

He did not know. Phyllis was, despite his own great powers, a violent and dangerous person. While it was important that he call the Piper at the earliest opportunity, the General would understand the delay. *I would have contacted you sooner, General, but dangerous emanations in the stratosphere prevented me from doing so!*

Not even a few placid days on Coney Island helped Phyllis remember who she was, or where she had come from, or who was after her.

It was amnesia. It preyed upon her. It seemed that her memory was a brimming vessel, rich with her past, but she could not open it. It was sealed almost tight. She could recall a few things with less than certainty. She thought that perhaps she had been a ballet dancer. And a prostitute. Her father had not lived in Florida, but elsewhere, and he might be dead. In New York she remembered a black woman telling her to stay away from pimps, yet sending her to a man who was like a pimp. Perhaps he had told her a story about Delancey Street, a stop on the subway. Prostitutes, a bridge. What had she been doing in Florida? How had she come to know Teddy? She had a tattoo on her wrist which represented what men wanted her to be, and how she should answer. *Vera.* But that was not her name.

From Teddy she tried to find out more, but he was evasive.

"I just met you, that's all."

"What about the Piper?"

"You'll find out." He smirked.

He wouldn't even talk about himself. Sometimes he said he came from Duluth, Iowa, but just as often he played smart aleck and said he was from the planet Quexquar. She wanted to shake him until the truth came out.

"Where are you from?"

"Where do *you* come from?" he laughed at her.

"Where's your mother? your father?"

"Quex—"

She hardly even remembered how it had been when they had lived together before the old man had died. In a basement, eating food, sleeping, a television. Teddy seemed to know more than she did, then. Now the tables had turned somehow. But what did she know?

"You're crazy," he liked to tell her. "Free and crazy."

At times she wanted to leave him. She could take what money was left and go. Yet there were moments when Teddy seemed to rupture and expose himself. He needed her then, when he wept, when he told her to stab him—whenever she threatened him. She knew also that he longed for her sometimes. She could feel him even while he lay a few feet away from her, on the bed, with his arms fallen over his eyes, while the television babbled on.

"Do you want me to lie down?"

"I don't care," he said coolly.

She would lie beside him; she could feel his perceptible relief. Late at night when even the TV was off, Teddy liked to wake up and watch her sleep. She knew this, and several times she caught him at it. The light of a street lamp, and one night a harvest moon, was cast across her body, and her eyes opened suddenly and found him staring.

"What is it?"

"Nothing." He lay down and turned away.

"Do you want to hold me?"

"No. Of course not."

On Saturday Fritz Elysis had been dead one week. To celebrate, Phyllis and Teddy played videogames at a restaurant on the Boardwalk. They spent a ten dollar bill. It was their last.

TWENTY-SEVEN

On Sunday morning a fuzzy but recognizable photograph of Phyllis Lantern, taken from the video image, appeared in the *Daily News,* the day after the last installment of Lucas's articles. It was in a little box by itself, beside a short dispatch concerning the grand jury about to convene in Florida, to which Sylvia Barnes was expected to testify that she didn't know what her son did or where he was spending his time. The caption read:

Police have tentatively identified the girl in this photograph as Phyllis Lantern, 14, one of the alleged victims of the sexual bondage ring known as the Pipeline. Anyone with information on her whereabouts should contact police at this special number. . . .

Lucas reasoned that it was a calculated risk. In the minds of the Piper and his cub, it would firmly link him to the girl.

"They'll kill her for sure," said Roscoe Gatling, "if they find her before you do."

"They may already have her," agreed Lucas. They stood outside the Daily News Building watching the morning editions being loaded onto the trucks. Phyllis's picture was on page 5.

Gatling shrugged. "They probably won't even see it. Who knows?"

"Maybe they've already left the country."

"Then they can hire a hit man like they did with— what was her name?"

"Vera." Lucas grimaced. "They're all named Vera."

"Well, Phyllis is lucky," said Gatling, shaking his head. "Lucky that somebody like you is watching out for her."

"Somebody has to."

"I bet you'll just be sitting home today, waiting for the phone to ring."

"I have call forwarding," said Lucas. "But yeah, that's right."

"Well, I'd sit around and wait with you, but . . ."

"That's all right."

"My wife gets out of the hospital tomorrow. I got to clean up the house and hide the gefilte fish."

"I understand."

In fact, Jonathan Barnes and Luis Barrezia had made reservations to leave New York as early as October 22, the day after they arrived. But, because Teddy didn't call after Fritz Elysis's demise, they kept pushing back the date. In this way they had exasperated several travel agents. They planned to join an innocuous charter flight to Freeport, hire a private plane to the Grand Bahamas, swim, and make arrangements for Paraguay at their leisure. Their false passports were in order.

Ostensibly, they were waiting for Teddy's call because they wanted to protect Sylvia's flank—so to speak. But there was another reason they remained all week in New York. They were having a good time.

Oh, it was a disaster, certainly—Jonathan and the Cuban agreed. The whole kids' show was disrupted, uprooted, and the money lost—as though lucre had ever been their motive—was incalculable. But it was also beautiful. They had not been so close in years.

What better companion, thought Jonathan, than Luis Barrezia? Over breakfast on Sunday morning, at the famous old van Dyck's restaurant on 43rd Street and Eighth Avenue, they perused the *Daily News*. Barrezia poured his coffee carefully over the picture of Phyllis Lantern.

"Like acid rain, no?"

Jonathan shook his head. "Lucas Jameson—we should've known all along."

"We? You should know have been Lucky Jimsom! We play Castro speaks—''

"Not now."

The Cuban smiled. "Later."

They sat in the green vinyl booth, side by side, and ordered omelettes and minute steaks, crisp bacon and pork sausage, and plenty of toast with coffee. They had always enjoyed eating together.

"We met for the first time over a meal," Jonathan pointed out.

Barrezia laughed and put his napkin to his mouth. "This is true, yes!"

"We weren't eating it, that's true."

"Was dog!"

Barrezia nodded vigorously and slipped a piece of bacon into his mouth. "Bow-wow."

"You'd make a good dog," noted Jonathan.

"Yes," said Barrezia. "When intestines come out, let me know."

"I will. Sylvia can make little purses out of them, and sell them—"

"In the streets, to passersby—yes!" Barrezia held up a pork sausage. "Excuse, please, madam. Would you like to buy a little purse made out of the intestines of Jonathan Barnes?"

Jonathan splayed his hands across his forehead to make a woman's hat. In a high voice he exclaimed: "Intestinal purses by Jonathan Barnes! How lovely!"

What they said was true. They had met over a meal.

On a warm autumn evening in Miami, in 1965. Chance alone had brought them to the same spot: one of the ocean-front parks along Collins Avenue. Chance—and the screams. From separate directions they had followed the sound of a man in agony. And a little crowd had gathered in the park, near the parapet where the beach ends.

"Somebody better do something," said a bystander. "Call the police! Somebody!"

An old derelict lay on the pavement. His stomach had been sliced open with a straight razor. He was the victim of some small dispute concerning money or a half-pint of sweet wine.

As he writhed in agony, the squeamish among the crowd disappeared into the night. Jonathan and Luis drifted together, as close as they could get without offering to help.

A stray dog was soon attracted by the scent of blood. There were many such strays then, and they usually ate hotel garbage. This was a mangy German shepherd. He wagged his tail and sniffed at the wounded man. Playfully he began pulling at the old derelict's entrails. And eating them.

It was beautiful to watch. Jonathan hunkered down, and Barrezia licked his lips and perspired.

The derelict wanted only to die. He screamed that someone should shoot him. The dog barked and wanted to play, and growled and pulled at the grey mass of intestine.

Finally the police came. Jonathan heard the sirens and felt the flashing light upon his back. His heart sank. Beside him Barrezia bit his lip:

"God damn! *El radiador tiene un escape—*"

"Oh my Jesus!" cried softly one of the police, who later could be heard vomiting behind the parapet.

The other cop sized up the situation quickly. He touched the Cuban on the shoulder and pulled his gun.

"Yes," nodded Barrezia gravely. "I will be witness."

The old man's head recoiled as the cop put two bullets in it. Frightened by the gunfire, the dog ran away.

"I was aiming for the dog," said the cop. "You're my witness."

Jonathan and Barrezia remained after the other onlookers had left. The ambulance came and took away the body. The fire department arrived and hosed down the bloody pavement. Barrezia said his first words to Jonathan:

"Did you see kidney?"

Jonathan inclined his head. "Yes."

"Tengo sed! I'm thirsty."

They left the scene and had drinks together on the veranda at the Fountainbleau. Jonathan was only seventeen, a keen student of mathematics at Florida State. The week before he had been to a party at the home of his anthropology professor—an ill-fated day! Luis Barrezia, nearly thirty, was a veteran of the Bay of Pigs, or, as he called it, the Battle of Girón. He had been thrown out of medical school before leaving Havana. He had been looking forward to the anatomy course.

Despite the disparity of backgrounds, they had talked late into the night. What if it had been a woman instead of a man? What if the woman were young rather than old? What if there had been two dogs, and they had fought over the entrails? Or, perhaps, copulated?

And toward morning they staggered through the Miami streets and picked up an old whore on a streetcorner. They brought her to a hotel. Although she was large enough to accept both of them at once, Jonathan opted merely to watch. Beneath a bare light bulb and oblivious to the rising sun, the Cuban mounted her from behind, and as he climaxed, he glanced back to an intent Jonathan Barnes, crying:

"We are fast friends!"

At four o'clock that cold Sunday afternoon, Jonathan Barnes and Luis Barrezia walked across 45th Street to the Film Center Cafe.

"Teddy must call today," said the Cuban.

"We must kill the girl," nodded Jonathan.

"But Jonathan! How does one kill something so beautiful as she?"

The streets were crowded with matinee goers. Limousines and buses were parked everywhere. As they passed the Martin Beck Theater, Jonathan noted with satisfaction that once again the marquee spoke to him with elliptical simplicity. It was the Royal Shakespeare Company's production of *All's Well That Ends Well*. He smiled with hope, and answered his friend:

"With a sledgehammer?"

TWENTY-EIGHT

$500 had seemed like a lot of money when they had taken it. But bus rides, the boarding house, a television, Coney Island amusements—all these things, not to speak of food and comics—had depleted it. Phyllis had seen it dwindling but just hadn't wanted to think about it. And now they were broke.

Phyllis knew what she had to do. She had a profession, it seemed, but she hadn't been practicing it. So had Teddy. On Sunday afternoon they counted their money, and it was only a few dollars in change that they sprinkled over the bed. As she sat staring on the bed, he came over to her with one hand on his hip.

"You want me to hustle?"

"No." She pulled down his hand.

"What'll we do then?"

"I'll take care of it."

"You're gonna hustle then, right?"

"Maybe."

He grinned. "You want me to pimp for you?"

"No."

"What are we—"

They were interrupted by the landlady, knocking at the door. She wanted her rent, and they were already a day late. Phyllis had already offered her Teddy's gold watch, but she didn't think it was real and turned it down.

"Give us another day?" asked Phyllis politely.

The old woman smelled of cat litter and beer. She raised a finger. "One day," she croaked. "Then I lock you out."

But then there was the problem of Teddy. In the week since they'd come to New York, she'd hardly left him alone for a minute. He hadn't called the Piper, but only because she hadn't given him the chance. Once he had tried, but she'd caught him. Those were the times that Phyllis wanted to kill him, wanted to wrap his head in a plastic bag and watch him suffocate. His tongue would come out. What was he going to do if she went off turning tricks?

"I won't try anything," he promised. "It's okay."

She didn't believe him. But what could she do? In the late afternoon she fixed him something to eat before she left. She presented him with a couple of comic books, too, that she had saved until now. And she made him go to the bathroom, telling him:

"You can use the sink when I'm gone, if you have to."

He seemed unconcerned about everything. In a too casual voice he asked, "When'll you be back?"

"About midnight."

"Okay," he shrugged. "Where are you going?"

It seemed to Phyllis that she could go anywhere there were prostitutes. There were plenty in Coney Island, but that made her uncomfortable. In Manhattan she knew—*how* she knew she couldn't have said—there was Third Avenue, Eighth Avenue, Tenth Avenue. And Delancey Street, the route across the bridge. When she thought about it, that seemed best. Blowjobs, that was all she had to do on the bridge. No hassles with hotels—

"Delancey Street," she shrugged.

"How far is that?"

"Not far, I don't think."

Teddy lay down on the bed and picked up a comic book. "I'll see you then."

For a moment she paused. She was gazing at herself in the mirror over the sink. She had only lipstick, no other makeup. She couldn't say if she looked pretty or not, but she knew she looked like a whore and—suddenly—that Teddy was jealous.

She turned and said, "You don't want me to go."

He shrugged. "I don't care."

She went around the bed to face him. He looked up, and saw her, and turned around. "Teddy—"

"Get out," he said. "Just go."

She tried to touch him, to make him face her, but he refused. "We need the money."

"That's right."

She shrugged. And left. With the old steel key she locked him in. As she went downstairs, she stopped by the landlady's door and took a folded five-dollar bill out of her shoe. She had been saving it. When the old woman came to the door, Phyllis said, "I have to go pick up the rent money. My brother's in the room still, but I don't want him going anywhere. Help me out, all right?"

The woman dropped the bill into her bosom and shut the door. She said not a word, not even a thank-you.

About five-thirty on Sunday afternoon Phyllis Lantern caught the subway to Manhattan. On the map she found where she was—Stillwell Avenue, Coney Island—and she put a finger on where she was going. The stop was easy to find. It was Delancey Street, just across the Williamsburg Bridge.

After Phyllis left, Teddy lay inert in bed for quite some time. He had decided not to call the Piper. He didn't know exactly why. He had been waiting so long, and now it was easy to call, but he didn't care to. For a while he tried to fire himself up with communiqués. *General, I have just been informed* . . . But they were dull and uninspired.

Instead, he kept thinking about Phyllis. He couldn't get her out of his head. Although she was dangerous, Teddy had come to think that, in some ways, she was also necessary to his survival. Without her he might die. Of course, it was important—the General would agree—to withstand the threat of even death, but why invite it? Who had made him a sandwich, just moments ago, the taste of it still lingering in his mouth? Who had told him he should go to the bathroom, and informed him that he could use the sink while she was gone? Who had assured him that she didn't want to stab him? And who—who didn't want Teddy to call the Piper?

They were all one and the same person. Phyllis. Even while he pictured the brotherly smile of Luis Barrezia, Teddy wondered *Who?* And thought: he'd waited this long, why not a little longer?

And then, when he tried to read a comic, all he could think was that she was out hustling. Teddy was upset. For a while he watched the fish swimming in the bowl. Hustling. It had never bothered him before. When he had watched old Fritz, the sick fucker, screw Phyllis, he hadn't cared in the slightest. He had no idea where Delancey Street was, but he imagined that men much like Fritz were approaching her— even as he, Teddy, watched the goldfish. It made him sick. He lay down.

He could see them following her up the steps of some enormous, dark hotel. They pinched her on the stairs. They watched as she undressed and then she was lying down on the bed with her legs spread. She was shaved. Afterwards she was crying. Teddy could see himself in the room with her. He was saying to the old men, "She's had enough. Don't fuck her any more. Let me take her." He was helping her get dressed. Her face was red from tears and her hair disheveled. "Thanks," she was saying, as he handed her a stocking. "Let's go," he was telling her. "I'll get you out of here."

She was crying and laughing at the same time. She was so grateful.

*   *   *

This frame of mind lasted in Teddy until about seven-thirty that Sunday evening. By then he was nearly insane with jealousy, but since he seldom felt anything at all, he was enjoying it in a way. He pushed the Piper out of his mind.

The television was still turned on. The news was showing. Teddy never watched the news. He was staring blankly at the screen and thinking of Phyllis, when suddenly a picture of her came on the screen.

He sat bolt upright.

"This fourteen-year-old girl," the newsman was saying, "is Phyllis Lantern. She was abducted last April from New York City and, according to the *Daily News,* forced into sexual bondage. Now police are saying that she may have escaped her captors. They are asking anyone with information about Phyllis to call this number: two-one-two . . ."

Teddy rose from the bed. He had been lounging half-naked in just his shirt. He put on pants and some shoes. He washed his face and hands, then combed his hair. From the bed he claimed the loose change. He picked up a kitchen knife and went to the door, made his first of several attempts to unlock it.

I am coming, General! I can hear your voice across the galaxies, and I am coming with all due speed!

TWENTY-NINE

For Sunshine it was one of those aggravating Sundays. It was slow, it was cold, a wind was up, and it even looked like it might snow. And when she got back to Moisha's after a trip across the Williamsburg Bridge in a cream-colored Lincoln Continental, a derelict ran into her headlong and spilled sweet wine all over her short skirt. She knocked him in the teeth, she was so aggravated.

"And this guy I just did was a paper salesman, too," she told the counterman. She wiped her skirt with a paper towel dunked in a glass of water. "Kimberly-Clark. Give me a coke, for Christ's sake."

The restaurant was moist and warm, stuffy with the smell of old grease. Sunshine saw only a few acquaintances, but it was early yet. Mostly there was Ingrid, decked out in a magenta dress that ended above her knees. She weighed three hundred pounds. She was drunk. Earlier she had been sitting at the counter eating doughnuts, but now she was up. Her eyes closed beneath sparkling lids, she was dancing in the middle of the floor by the cash register. And singing to herself:

> *Church, I'm full saved today—*
> *Fully saved today!*
> *I am in that narrow way—*
> *That narrow way!*

Coke in hand, Sunshine watched Ingrid a while. She had always liked spirituals. Then she walked to the back, where the tables were almost empty. Her only company was a little whore whom she had never seen before. The girl was drinking coffee and smoking, and her face was ashen except for bright lipstick. She was a young one. She was dressed in jeans, a pink sweater, and only a levi jacket.

"I bet you're cold," said Sunshine.

"Yeah."

"I haven't seen you before."

The girl sipped her coffee and shook her head. Very uncommunicative.

Sunshine added, "Look what happened to my skirt."

"What is it?"

"Wine. Some fucking bum. It'll never come out right. You got the best idea. Wear jeans."

The girl nodded vaguely. "It's windy out there," she said, rolling curled fingers against her cheek. "Is it always this windy?"

"Only on nights when the wind blows," said Sunshine. "These are nights you bring knitting. You ever knit?"

"No."

"I used to work knitting. I mean, sewing. In a factory. They had a pedal you pushed on the floor. But something went wrong with my nerve down there. In your foot you got the longest nerve in your body. Sciatica, they called it. When I'd press my foot down there, I could feel it up here."

"I never had that yet."

Phyllis drained her coffee. It was almost nine o'clock at night and she had turned just one trick. The flat taste was in her mouth and wouldn't go away. She could still feel his hand on the back of her head. It was a familiar feeling. She'd got twenty dollars, most of it still in her pocket. If she didn't get more, she and Teddy were going to have to move somewhere else. Maybe, she thought, they ought to in any case. They ought to get out of New York altogether. She had been in this city before, but it wasn't helping her memory any to be back. She said idly:

"I used to be a dancer."

"Yeah—me, too."

Phyllis glanced at the woman sharply. The sardonic smile caught her off-guard. She rose suddenly, awkwardly.

"Listen, I didn't mean anything." Sunshine caught

the girl by the wrist, her hand covering the tattoo. "You going out now, honey?"

"Yeah." Phyllis nodded. "I better."

"Well, pick me up a paper if you see one, okay?"

"Okay."

"A *Daily News*." Sunshine smiled. "I'll give you the money."

THIRTY

"When time gets hard and evil triumphs, what is the task of the good man?"

Teddy thought for a moment. *"To stay the course?"*

Luis Barrezia took a deep breath. He clasped the shoulder of Jonathan Barnes, standing next to him in the telephone booth. The barflies at the Film Center Cafe were watching the harness races. Jonathan heaved a sigh of relief.

It seemed to the Cuban that he and Teddy could profitably dispense with the rest of the programmed conversation.

"Where are you, Teddy?"

"To send her to heaven . . ."

Barrezia pinched the bridge of his nose.

"Vahalia!"

Patiently but firmly Barrezia said, *"Teddy Dray. The General has a special message for Teddy Dray. Is he listen?"*

A pause, then: "Yes, Luis?"

"Tell me where you are located, please."

The Cuban's voice was warm and the command firm. When Teddy heard it, a surge of masculine relief passed through him. Why had he waited so long? he wondered.

"Coney Island," said Teddy. "Do you wish our exact address?"

Barrezia smiled into the receiver. "Is Phyllis with you, Teddy?"

"No, she's . . ."

He had a moment of uncertainty. Did he have to tell Luis what he had let her do? Would the General be angry that he had let her out of his sight? He said:

"I couldn't help it, I—"

"Where is she, please?"

"On Delancey Street giving blowjobs," said Teddy in one rushing breath. "She went there today. She's there right now. I couldn't stop her. I tried. She hurt me . . ."

"Is all right," said Barrezia firmly. It was important to know how to deal with a boy's anxiety.

"She's—"

"One moment, please, Teddy. Very important orders coming up down Pipeline in one second."

The Cuban clamped a hand over the mouthpiece and looked to Jonathan for guidance. "She's on Delancey Street. Now."

"Tell him to meet us there," said Jonathan.

"How I tell him? Now at Coney Island."

Jonathan shrugged. For all his trips to New York, he didn't know much about getting around by subway. He walked over to the bartender and asked, quite casually, where to find girls downtown. He asked a couple of other questions before he returned.

"Tell him to take the F train to Delancey Street. We'll meet him outside Ratner's Delicatessen. Best challah in town." He shook his head. "Whatever that is."

Luis Barrezia pointed to the inside of the telephone. "To convey very difficult."

Jonathan raised his eyebrows. "Jail very long."

"This is General Luis Barrezia with important message for Theodore Dray—"

On Times Square, even on a Sunday evening, it was easy to purchase a knife. Luis Barrezia decided that he wanted one.

"It's been many years," said Jonathan, "since I've seen you with a knife."

"Many years," nodded Barrezia, "since I go cutting up little girls."

"To be protected from violence against one's person is a basic human right," said Jonathan, deadpan.

The Cuban pointed to the Bowie knife. He did not believe the clerk's assurances that it was sharp, and tested it against a hair from Jonathan's head.

"This is what New York is doing to me," said Jonathan.

"Very sharp," nodded Barrezia. He paid cash. It came with a holster. "No need to wrap," he told the clerk.

Before they took a cab downtown, Jonathan called Sylvia. It was, for once, a pleasure to hear her voice. It was like honey. He smiled and said:

"Do you know who this is?"

"Why, I certainly do!" Sylvia gushed. "How're you doing?"

"Everything is swell. We're on our way."

"Show me the way to go home?"

Jonathan smiled and began to sing softly into the telephone:

> *Show me the way to go home*
> *I'm tired and I want to go to bed*
> *I had a little drink about an hour ago*
> *And it went right to my head*

Sylvia joined in for the second verse:

> *Wherever I may roam*
> *Be it land or sea or foam*
> *You can always hear me singing this song*
> *Show me the way to go home*

There were tears in Jonathan's eyes when they finished. He asked her:

"What about you?"

"Oh," laughed Sylvia, "it just seems like people

are asking me all kinds of questions. They want to know every little thing.''

"I bet they do," he nodded.

"You got anything more to tell me, sweetie?''

Jonathan thought hard. There was a lump in his throat. He didn't know when he'd next see her. He said, "I—I bought you some of that lotion. I'll bring it with me the next time I come.''

"That'll be just wonderful," chortled Sylvia. "Just dandy!''

Jonathan walked out of the booth staring.

"How is Sylvia?'' asked the Cuban. He raised a hand to hail a taxi.

"Fine.'' Jonathan looked up at the Cuban. "I got her some of that lotion.''

THIRTY-ONE

Phyllis Lantern was sighted about three dozen times on Sunday, not only in New York but also in New Jersey, Connecticut, and Rhode Island. Apparently there was no shortage of young, desolate blondes in the Northeast. But the real Phyllis was not noticed by anybody. Lucas Jameson was not devoid of hope, but he tried, as the evening wore on, to accustom himself to the inevitable.

"Maybe she's dead."

"Or they might kill her."

"Yes, they . . ."

Louise Cole stood beside Lucas at the bar in the Venus Lounge. She eyed him warily. With a curled finger she pointed to the picture in the *Daily News* that was spread out in front of her.

"If she's dead, she's dead—that's all."

Lucas nodded, tightlipped. The old woman was displeased with him. She had been simmering all evening. She didn't approve of his having the photo published. Even less did she appreciate his traipsing through her bar, his feet muddied with self-disgust.

"If you hate yourself, Mr. Jameson," she had asked him quietly, early on, "why don't you keep it to yourself?"

"Sorry." He leaned against the bar like a stick of dung.

She quaffed a cognac and pushed a straight green Pernod into his hand. "How long have I been knowing you, Mr. Jameson? Six months?"

He nodded.

"Six months, and I would say—it isn't anything personal—that you're not really such a lovely person."

"No."

"It's been dawning on me."

"Did you ever think so?"

"No." Louise closed the newspaper and pushed it away. "But it takes one to know one. Who sent you the girl, anyway?"

"You did."

The old woman nodded. "And now she's lost. What'd you think was gonna happen to her? You think Big Chief—Piper; they're all the same—you think these men wouldn't slit her throat and buy a necklace after? What are you worried about?''

He shrugged. Perhaps if he knew for a fact that she was dead, he might've stood it better. The uncertainty plagued him. Her picture on the television and in the newspaper danced grotesquely in his head. *Maybe I'm alive, Lucas*. He wanted her to live. He wanted to see her again, to hold her again. But the very possibility taunted him.

"All right," said Louise. "Say they kill her. You can't do anything about it. Not now. You mighta thought of it in the first place."

Lucas looked lamely into his drink. The old woman had been after him like this all night. "My consc—"

"And don't tell me about your goddamned conscience!" she screamed at him. Two aspirin appeared before her on the bar; with a glass of water she swallowed them and set down the glass with a tiny thud. "If you start worrying about conscience, you're nothing more than an animal."

He sighed with exasperation, impotence.

"I spent fifteen—twelve—years in the racket," said Louise, "and didn't know nothing about no conscience."

"No, I—"

"And neither do you."

He spoke into his drink. "No."

"You're just like one of them Voodoo dolls, Mr. Jameson." Louise looked upon a new cognac, as if even she was surprised the glass was full again. "People stick pins in you—you don't care. You cause people harm and trouble—you don't give a damn. And open you up—what's inside?" The old lady took a drink. "Nothing but a mess of crap."

"Thanks."

"What?"

"I said, thanks."

"You walk in looking hang-dog waiting for a telephone call about where is Phyllis Lantern."

He glanced at the clock above her head. It was past nine o'clock.

"You sit at my bar and I buy your drinks and all you can tell me is you got a motherfucking conscience."

Lucas had to gather a certain temerity just to look at her, in fact. And when he did, he saw she was pouting. What was she like in 1929? Tonight the mask of gentility had come off. She stood at the bar with one foot up, one hand on her hip and the other gone in the shirring of her gown. She turned her eyes up to him like a twenty-year-old, and when he averted his eyes, she said:

"Look at me."

Those three little words shuttled through his ears like so many howling wolves. Why indeed should Lucas Jameson look at anybody? At anybody but monks immolated by fire and the victims of searing disaster? Or at the dead eyes of Westchester addicts or little girl slaves?

"Why don't you just admit it?" asked Louise.

"What?"

"That you loved the girl and it don't matter if she's fourteen or any age? What stops you?"

He shook his head.

"It's not your conscience. Don't tell me that." She reached for his hand. "I can see why—"

"No, you—"

"The lightning wants to come out your fingers,"

she said. And reached for his mouth. "And to breathe fire like a dragon."

He stood there, sweating, in a rage.

The telephone rang.

THIRTY-TWO

*As I emerged from the starship, the General was
waiting for me with his aide-de-camp, Sir Jonathan
Barnes!*

They were standing in the shadows of a restaurant.
The kindly Barrezia, in a gentle white suit, and the
slight, bespectacled dynamo, Barnes, hardly disguised
by a growth of beard. Teddy did not run to greet
them, but walked calmly, hands in pockets, with

266

casual dignity. He smiled and inclined his head when Luis hunkered down to receive him.

It was a pleasure to see the General.

"Now," said Barrezia, taking the boy by the shoulders, "we have some business to conduct."

"What?"

"Where is Phyllis?"

Teddy shrugged. "Around here somewhere."

They were quite near the bridge. Delancey Street was only a half-dozen short blocks long. A wide street with a central divider, it was bounded on the south by abandoned tenements and on the north by cheap shops of all kinds, all shuttered by corrugated steel and padlocked. On Sunday night it was almost deserted. The wind sprayed paper and nudged empty bottles; the derelicts lay inert.

"We wish must to find her," smiled the Cuban. He turned the boy around and spoke into his ear. "We take a walk."

Teddy nodded. He understood. Suddenly he turned around. *"Vahalia!"* he smiled.

Barrezia nodded. "Please, Teddy. Walk."

As the General rose I could see—

"Let's get going," said Jonathan Barnes, emerging from the shadows.

He began to walk. Yet Teddy's pace was off, his swagger awry. He felt dizzy. *And within his coat was a—*

"Good, Teddy. Keep going."

The boy could not evade the impression that he had seen a knife in the General's jacket. The handle had been visible, and the leather sheath.

"We are looking for Phyllis, Teddy," said the General.

"It is very important to find her," said Sir Jonathan.

"Walter, Walter—what are you doing with that knife?" said his mother.

Jonathan and Barrezia walked behind the boy by twenty paces. Teddy would see the girl first. If she intended to escape, Teddy would hold her. But repeatedly the boy stopped, turned around . . .

General, allow me to—

"Obey orders, Teddy. Very important. Do not turn around."

"Aye, aye, General. But allow me to ask you a question about the knife in your—

As he walked, the wind was at his back, like the breath of the galaxies. Where was Phyllis? he wondered. Was the knife intended for her? *Don't fuck her any more she's had enough. You're so grateful you're crying and laughing at the same time I love you Mommy Walter what are you doing with that knife?*

"Where is she?" wondered the Cuban.

"We'll find her," said Jonathan.

Phyllis was at Moisha's Diner, about five blocks away. She had just upset the table at which she had been sitting with a prostitute named Sunshine. Their coffee cups lay broken. The *Daily News* was strewn across the floor. A picture of Phyllis Lantern stared up at Phyllis Lantern—but she didn't care. In fact, all she could do was scream at Sunshine:

"You called me Phyllis!"

Sunshine had dodged the falling table, but got coffee sprayed on her skirt. What a lousy night. The girl was wild-eyed. Sunshine pointed to the newspaper:

"I just wanted to show—"

"I said my name was *Sandy!*" the girl hissed.

"But honey—"

"And you made a telephone call—didn't you?" Phyllis pointed an accusing finger. "I *saw* you. Who were you calling? It was about *me*, wasn't it?"

In fact, Sunshine had called Lucas about five minutes before. And he had begged her to keep the girl at the restaurant, nothing more. She owed him a favor, and now she was about to blow it. In all innocence—never her strong suit—she said:

"I—I just had to make a call. What's eating you? I make plenty—"

"Get away from me."

Sunshine was edging closer, and almost whispering. "Look, honey, at your wrist." She turned up her own. "The tattoo—"

Phyllis made a sudden dash, and Sunshine followed. She caught the girl, too, by the coat. Phyllis screamed and scrambled through the chairs, dragging the woman with her. The walls at Moisha's were filled with murals of Tel Aviv. Sunshine had never been so close to Ben-Yehuda Street as when Phyllis pushed her. She lost her balance and slipped to the floor. She cut her lip on the way down. She wanted to cry out, *Get her!*—but hands to capture grit were not quick at Moisha's.

The girl dashed unmolested into the street. Ingrid never missed a beat.

> I know his blood can make me whole—
> No evil can betide
> I'm walking in that narrow way!

Phyllis ran virtually into the arms of Lucas Jameson. He was just getting out of a taxi. For a second she stopped, uncertain which direction to take. He stepped toward her—

"*Phyllis*—"

Everybody knew her name.

He caught her by the arms when she tried to run. He pulled her back and wouldn't let her go. He repeated her name—*Phyllis, Phyllis, Phyllis*—while she started screaming.

"Don't—" he tried to calm her: "Don't scream."

That was what they all said.

"*I'm Lucas—Lucas*—"

She focused on his strange face for a second. Lucas. Lucas. Lucas.

Never saw him before in her life.

"*Let me go!*"

He saw the animal violence in her eyes—the wild, trapped and escape-from-death blue eyes that looked into his without memory. And he was mute.

Her lips were twisting, spitting. And his heart closed up, veins and all.

She wrenched free of his hands. And ran.

She could hear him behind her then. He ran with a limp, it seemed, and could not go fast. He kept calling her name. Once she looked back. He was following her with a palm pressed to a thigh, his face contorted. She had never seen him before. He was a pimp. She could tell. He was disgusting. *License plates. Every question of risk. Quad Cities. You may get killed. Glenn Miller was already dead. Music is a dying profession. If you let the pigs fuck you* WHERE WILL IT ALL END?

She fled from him down Delancey Street, ran for the Williamsburg Bridge that lay ahead with its lights blinking through the mist. She was five—four—three blocks away from it. She had no idea where she was going when she blinked and blinked and saw:

Teddy.

What was he doing here? What form of transport? Was she imagining him? He stood before her on the sidewalk, just a few yards away, gazing at her. Not much of a friend, but who else was there? A smile played on his lips. She called out:

"Teddy! Teddy!"

And when she looked up to the bridge, she saw the way it seemed to go up into the sky. To the moon. She would take him there with her. The bridge to the sky to the moon and she reached out her hands—

"I'm being chas—"

She didn't break her gait, but pulled his head into her breast and dragged him along. But he forced her to stop. He was holding her hands.

"Chased, Teddy—chased!"

He was pulling her back. Still smiling. Gripping her now, holding her wrists. Smiling not at but behind her. Tightening his clasp and suddenly letting out a piercing cry—

"General! I have her I have her I have her!"

THIRTY-THREE

When Phyllis saw the Piper—and she did recognize him, as in a nightmare repeated—she tried to pull herself free from Teddy. She was unsuccessful. He held on valiantly. He began to kick her. They fought in a dizzy arc on the sidewalk. Perhaps, if she had had another ten seconds, she could have broken free.

Then she heard their voices:

"Hold her yes, Teddy," said Barrezia.

"That's right," said Jonathan. "Don't let her go."

Lucas Jameson was still about thirty yards away. He was crossing Essex Street and got in the way of a speeding car which, unfortunately, missed him. He was limping, and each time he came down on his left foot—the same foot which Quinta Mechanic had broken for him months before—he received a fresh jolt of pain.

Ahead he saw the bizarre dance between Phyllis and the boy. He heard the boy's shrill cry—and now he saw the two men emerge in the night. The Cuban looked like an enormous owl.

He could never reach them in time if they were quick. When he saw the knife, his mind went blank with rage. He didn't break his stride.

Barrezia walked toward her with the knife hanging from the hand dropped loosely at his side. To Phyllis he addressed himself with a smile:

"Hello, little one."

THIRTY-FOUR

Quinta Mechanic was sitting in the front seat of a taxicab parked at the very foot of Delancey Street. This put her at about a block away from the action. She had been following Barnes and Barrezia ever since four o'clock that afternoon, when they had walked from the Milford Plaza to the Film Center Cafe. She had watched the Cuban buy a knife. Her taxi had followed theirs downtown.

"This is it," said Quinta.

Her cab driver was a young Iranian named Massoud Singh Sharma. He was small, with jet black hair and a delicate face. Quinta thought that he possessed a surprisingly agile mind. He knew from the Shah; he knew from Khomeini. It seemed that he had lived in France for quite some time before coming to America. He agreed with Quinta about the Eiffel Tower. And now she pointed ahead and hissed:

"Let's go, Swami!"

Quinta had already told him how she wanted him to swerve around the car parked in front of them and skid to a stop at curbside. Massoud had been agreeable up to now.

"Over there it very dangerous!"

Quinta waited for him to fire the ignition. He did nothing of the kind.

"Step on it."

"I no go—"

Quinta was suddenly inarticulate. She grasped him by the collar of his jacket. *"Listen, you Islamic motherfucker—get a move on!"*

But Massoud shook his head resolutely. He withdrew the keys from the ignition.

Just then she wanted to kill him. She could hear the girl screaming. She had planned something beautiful.

"It no good," said Massoud. "It very bad."

She let go of his collar. What good did it do to get angry? Quinta wagged a finger at him.

"Next time I see your mother," she said, "I'm going to—"

Rip off her veil. But Quinta didn't say it. She was already out of the cab. She tossed him a twenty dollar bill. Then softly, she shut the door.

· THIRTY-FIVE

Jonathan Barnes felt his heart pound and his nostrils ventilate. He wanted to be close. He wanted to see it. He wanted to smell it. He wanted . . .

Lucas Jameson, was it, limping down the street? None other. The Cuban saw him, too. As Barrezia took hold of the girl, he glanced over to Jonathan and, smiling, noted:

"Lucky Jimson, no?"

"Yes."

"Him next."

All they needed now was a stray dog.

Jonathan positioned himself to rush Lucas if the Piper didn't move fast enough. And Luis Barrezia moved with exquisite slowness. Teddy was still hanging on to the girl, even after Barrezia had her around the throat.

"No, Teddy, let her go—"

It was necessary for Barrezia to kick the boy in the stomach. Jonathan couldn't help smiling as Teddy grunted. Now the Cuban's knife was flashing. Jonathan felt transported. He anticipated the blood and thrilled to see the girl's contorted face. Transported he felt—literally. Upwards. An enormous arm wound around his neck like a great snake. He stopped being able to breathe.

"Barrezia!"

Luis Barrezia looked up, like a barber called to the telephone. The girl lay against his chest and the knife lay in his hand, ready to open her up.

"Are you going to cut up that girl?"

He smiled. "I cut up girl, yes."

"Then I'm going to break old Jonathan's neck," said Quinta Mechanic, modestly. "I'm going to snap it in two."

Massoud Singh Sharma. He glanced at himself in the rearview mirror. He had a beautiful face. But what good was it? *He just little guy. Why Quinta so mad at him? He no like Shah. No like Khomeini. No fucking pray five times a day pointing East. She think he coward. Tyranny must be in every form resisted. She say Next time I see your mother. But no see mother.*

*Khomeini bury his mother like chicken and shoot off
her head. He should best this remember—*

Massoud felt for the tire iron below the front seat.
Trembling, he gunned the taxi.

In Luis Barrezia's split second of contemplation,
Lucas Jameson came climbing onto his back like a
maniac. The knife went clattering to the pavement.
Barrezia cursed, in Spanish, and flung the girl away
with one hand. With the other he grasped Lucas by
the neck, pulled him over his shoulder, picked him
up and pushed his head into the stone wall of the
Bank of Commerce.

The knife fell near Teddy. Who saw an excellent
opportunity. He picked it up and—even though it
looked like Daddy's knife—he handed it back to the
Cuban.

"Here you are, General."

When she saw the knife again in Barrezia's hand,
Quinta tossed off Jonathan Barnes like a shot-put.
She had grown up, after all, in Brighton Beach. She
loved fighting a blade. She crouched and began to
circle.

Phyllis Lantern lay dazed on the pavement. She
was surprised to see a taxicab swerve between parked
cars like a cynical chariot and squeal to a halt. But
she got up, like it was very much expected, and
staggered toward it without thinking. The door opened
from the inside. She had been screaming all along,
and still was screaming at the top of her lungs.

Both Jonathan Barnes and Lucas Jameson followed
her. She pulled shut the door.

Where do they go?
Why do they go?

What becomes of them?

As the taxi started to jerk away from the curb, Jonathan flung himself at the door and tried to wrench it open. Inside Phyllis was hysterical.

Jonathan had to do it: he *had* to kill her himself. Sylvia would never forgive him if he let her go. He could see his mother's smiling face and her breasts bouncing and middle finger rising even as he hauled himself onto the taxi's rear end.

Massoud Singh Sharma groaned and plunged the accelerator to the floor. The taxi jackknifed into the traffic lane in Massoud's effort to toss Jonathan off. It did not succeed. The taxi went crashing into the divider fence. There it stopped.

Jonathan giggled. He climbed off and tried again to open the back door. To get at Phyllis. She had locked the door and it wasn't easy. But the window was still half open. First he stuck his hands inside, and then his head. He was laughing at her. He could see the tears trembling on her cheeks.

"My mother is an ecdysisisisisi!"

Massoud Singh Sharma got out of his taxi. He climbed on the running board in time to see Lucas Jameson hauling Jonathan out of the back window. He waved the tire iron and Lucas raised his hand. He tossed the iron and Lucas caught it. The two exchanged these words:

"Me just a little guy."

"Me, too."

Teddy now thought that perhaps, in returning the knife to the General, he had made a mistake. It also occurred to him that he had forgot to feed his gold-fish that day. But the knife bothered him more.

General, he wanted to say, *I am afraid of the weapon which you wield.* Little enough of this world inspired fear in Teddy Dray. He watched Quinta Mechanic circle the General.

General—

When Quinta had slipped, the Cuban had stabbed her in the leg. From her thigh ran a stream of blood which dripped off her pantleg onto the pavement.

Although there were no police as yet on Delancey Street, a few onlookers had gathered to watch the fight. Teenagers and derelicts mostly. They made no comment, but they watched in icy fascination.

Luis Barrezia felt himself getting edgy. This had all been very splendid, but it was time to get on with the business of getting out. Out of the country. He no longer saw the girl, but he felt certain that Jonathan would be taking good care of her. Then it was time they both leave. Hell with Lucky Jimsom. To Vahalia with Teddy. He began to make quick, thrusting movements with the blade, and as Quinta retreated from them, their circle widened. He thrust, feinted, switched hands, and caught Quinta on the forearm.

Teddy watched the knife stick. It made a whoosh sound, and the blood made drip on the ground. And when he looked to the General—the General was gone! In his place Teddy saw—

Walter—what are you doing with that knife? Walter—put down that knife. Walter, for the child's sake—

And the child Teddy went running between his parents. He wanted to take the knife away from his father. In doing so, the blade went entirely through his body and could be seen sticking out of his back.

Quexquar! Teddy Dray to Quexquar! Come in, Mommy! Daddy!

The Cuban lifted the child off the ground as he shrugged him off the blade and retrieved the knife. Teddy's body slipped to the sidewalk like it had never been alive. Yet the boy's lips were moving rapidly:

"Quexquarquexquarquexquar—"

Barrezia saw what he had done. *We are originators of shotgun boy.* But perhaps it was not so funny as first it seemed. For when he looked up, Quinta Mechanic was standing at her full height. Shaking her head.

On the street, near where the taxi had laid down its last tracks, Lucas Jameson was singlemindedly beating Jonathan Barnes to death. No lightning crackled at his fingertips, nor fire from his mouth, but the tire iron worked well enough. Jonathan did not die easily. He did not even lose consciousness until almost the end. For a brief second Lucas stopped to hear what was coming out of that voice box.

"Pantries should be full! All hands should be working! This is not an inconceivable thought!"

Quinta Mechanic stopped playing games. Perhaps, too, Teddy's death wracked the Cuban's nerves. But Quinta brought both hands up and, moving toward him, evaded a stabbing thrust, then grasped Barrezia's arm—the one which wielded the knife. She twisted and broke this arm. He still held onto the knife, which she confiscated. She put a knee into his belly and he doubled over. Picking up his head by the hair of his crown, she kicked him in the shins. His legs buckled. She went around him, stepped on the small of his back, and pulled back his head. She wiped the blade on his shoulder and looked up. There was a small audience.

"A woman's got to do what a woman's got to do."

Dancing and prancing, turning from Clinton onto Delancey, came a mongrel dog.

THIRTY-SIX

Then it was almost over.

Lucas Jameson flung down the tire iron and walked back across the street. There the boy Teddy lay stabbed to death and Luis Barrezia was crumpled on the pavement with his throat slit open. Rivulets of blood ran into the street. Luckily, there was a sewer grating nearby. It was into this grating that Quinta Mechanic dropped the knife.

Nodding at the big woman, Lucas sat down on the curb. She sat beside him. The teenagers and derelicts had dispersed. Now, in the distance, could be heard a police siren, as though someone had thought to call those troublemakers.

"I can't stay," said Quinta. "I got to be going."

Lucas nodded. He watched the blood drip from his nose and mouth into the gutter.

"Did you know Phyllis?"

"No," said Quinta. "Never had the pleasure."

And he looked up, as though the taxi might be there yet, wound back through a hole in time. It was not. It had sped off into the night. The fence was still crooked where it had crashed.

"She's gone now," he said laconically.

"You'll have to find her."

"Yes."

Quinta eyed him with dispassion as she rose. "I'll be seeing you.

And when he looked around, she was gone. The dog, a crusty black cur, trotted from body to body and then to him. There was blood on its snout. It licked his face happily. Lucas saw it through a gauze of tears. He said,

"She used to be a dancer."

Hardly anything is more pleasing to the eye than a great bridge, viewed from the approaches, as it strikes out against the sky. A good example is Manhattan's famous Williamsburg Bridge, once the longest suspension bridge in the world. It is a sight which even today should be on every tourist's agenda. Children, however, are not allowed to play upon the walkway. They should be discouraged from doing so, and the wise adult will report any breaches of conduct to the proper authorities. It is well known that happiness and good things accrue to those who follow the rules; unhappiness and misery to those who do not. The Williamsburg Bridge, which crosses the East River with a forceful presence, can prove dangerous to young and old alike.